END SCENE

ELISE FABER

END SCENE
BY ELISE FABER

END SCENE

Print ISBN-13: 978-1-946140-76-0
Ebook ISBN-13: 978-1-946140-75-3
Cover Art by Jena Brignola

LOVE, CAMERA, ACTION

Dotted Line

Action Shot

Close Up

End Scene

Meet Cute

ONE

Maggie

MY CELL VIBRATED JUST as the minister declared, "You may now kiss the bride."

Slipping out of my chair as Eden and Damon locked lips, but before they vacated the altar, I sprinted down the aisle and toward a tree, hustling behind it.

Only five people were currently *not* on Do Not Disturb.

Eden—who was currently otherwise occupied.

Three additional equally important clients. All of whom were either in attendance—and Pierce and Artie were not likely to be on the phone as they watched the bride and groom get hitched—or on the opposite side of the globe—and Talbot was probably sleeping.

The last was my father.

Who *never* called unless something was on fire, someone was bleeding out, or an asteroid was heading toward the planet.

I glanced at the screen, not realizing how much I'd been hoping it was Talbot with some earth-shattering crisis until I saw "Dad calling" flashing across the surface. "Shit," I muttered, swiping a finger and bringing it up to my ear. "Hi, Dad. Everything okay?"

"It's not Dad."

Hot then cold. Goose bumps on my arms. The past shoving its way firmly into my present because his voice was ice, and it broke my heart.

Aaron.

My *ex* Aaron.

My ex because *I'd* left.

"What's wrong?" I asked.

"Your father fell," Aaron said. "He's in the hospital."

"What?" I gasped, my head falling back against the tree, my heart pounding. "What happened?"

"He decided he had to shovel the driveway—"

"What?!" I repeated like an idiot. "But I hired someone to come and do that—"

Cold infiltrated the airwaves. "Except that *someone* didn't show up, and your father decided he couldn't wait for me to come over and do it."

So many things wrong with that statement.

Why the company I'd hired hadn't shown up, why Aaron would still be seeing my dad, why my father would think it was a good idea to go out and shovel his driveway at sixty-nine years old after surviving four heart attacks.

"Is he okay?"

"He needs surgery," Aaron snapped. "A hip replacement."

I gasped. "Oh, my God! I—"

Cheers erupted from the audience behind me, Damon and Eden probably making their way down the aisle.

"Never mind. I can tell you're busy. I shouldn't have called," Aaron said, still cold, still so similar to how he'd sounded when I'd told him I was leaving—moving to L.A., leaving Utah behind. So different from how he'd sounded when we'd been together. But I'd made his warmth disappear as easily as freshly baked cinnamon apple bread around my father.

My father.

Shit.

Eyes burning at the thought of him all alone in the hospital. "I'll be on the next pl—"

Another cheer, voices coming my way.

"Enjoy your party, Mags."

I'd been about to say I would be on the next plane home, but Aaron hung up.

And I was left with silence in my ear, a worried and aching heart . . . alone but somehow still surrounded by people.

Alone, but not.

That was fitting.

Sighing, I shoved my phone into my pocket and went to retrieve my coat and purse, thankful I never left home for any big event without my go-bag. Then I bypassed the bride and groom, not wanting to spoil their special day, jumped into my car, and headed to the airport, buying a ticket on the first flight to Utah.

To Aaron—

No. To my father.

Only my father. Because Aaron was strictly in the past. We were over. There wasn't a future for us.

I'd made certain of it.

But as the plane soared across the sky, closing the distance between present and past, I was having a hard time remembering *why* I'd made certain of it.

I missed him.

And I'd . . . never stopped loving him.

TWO

Maggie

I REALIZED PRETTY QUICKLY that I was unprepared for Utah weather.

Maybe that was because I was in a spaghetti strap dress that revealed more thigh than it covered, or maybe it was because my coat was not Rocky Mountain winter warm.

It had been near eighty in southern California at the wedding.

Lovely. Clear skies. A warm off-shore breeze.

Part of the reason I'd gladly traded Utah for California.

Warm weather for the majority of the year. No snow. No tornados. Yes, the odd earthquake. Yes, a regular fire season, with smoke sometimes clouding the horizon.

But I could also wear a mini-skirt in November, so really, I couldn't complain.

My feet, on the other hand, were complaining mightily.

Thankfully, I kept a go-bag in my trunk for just this type of occasion—my clients could create a lot of trouble with very little effort, and I needed to be prepared to jump on a flight at a moment's notice. So, even though I hadn't had time to change before running for the plane, and even though I definitely hadn't wanted to fight with the tiny bathroom on that plane, teetering in heels and trying to peel myself out of the dress, I knew that once I found a decent place to change, I'd been good to go.

I also knew from experience that the heels didn't come off before then.

Because if they did, they wouldn't make it *back* on.

And—cue shudder—I was not walking through the airport in bare feet.

The fasten seat belt indicator flashed back on, the flight attendant making the announcement that the plane's descent was coming, and we would soon be on the ground.

I was going to be back on the ground in Utah.

Good lord.

I'd moved to Los Angeles ten years ago, only returning to the state for my dad's birthday, for Christmas, to help him after his heart attacks, and . . . that was it.

Campbell, Utah had been my youth. A great place to grow up—safe, with good schools, perfect for a single dad to find a close-knit community to raise his daughter. It was just . . . I'd always dreamed of more, of bigger places with bright lights. I'd dreamed of the ocean and endless sunny days. I'd . . .

Dreamed.

And while I loved my dad, he hadn't been a good father.

I'd lacked many things growing up—simple affection, an "I love you," an "I'm proud of you," but I'd most especially been lacking a loving, supportive environment. Oh, we'd had food, I'd had a place to sleep, but I'd never had tenderness. And a little girl who'd lost her mom had needed tenderness.

Not to be.

He'd ordered me to move back to Utah many times over—no

clue why he'd even want me there after the way he'd treated me —but I also knew I would never go back. I loved my job, my clients, and the big community of non-judgmental friends who'd become my extended family in L.A.

I didn't want to be back in Utah.

I wanted to be in California, my toes in the sand, the breeze tangling my brown hair, making it feel a lot sexier and more exciting than just plain brown, and I wanted my dad to move there with me.

I'd been on him about the change for years now.

A fresh start for both of us. Sun and the ocean to wash away the past. A chance for us to have something real.

Plus, no snow to shovel. No driveways to slip and fall and break a hip. No—

Ranch. No open fields. No horses in the back pasture or grassy hills in the distance.

That was the part of Utah I missed.

Fresh summer peaches, juice dripping down my chin that I had wiped away with my forearm when I was younger, juice that was kissed away when I got old enough to sneak off with boys.

With *one* boy.

With Aaron.

Ugh. I didn't want to go down this mental rabbit hole, but it was hard to forget the boy, the teen, the man who'd been my first . . . everything.

First kiss. First time. First love. First—

The plane's tires hit the runway with a sharp bump, jarring me out of my thoughts, but unfortunately not before the final word crossed my mind.

Heartbreak.

That I'd caused.

"Shit," I muttered, drawing the attention of my seatmate, who smiled indulgently.

"Not the smoothest landing," the woman said as the airplane taxied.

"No," I agreed.

We departed the plane. I skipped baggage claim in lieu of a rental car, since my go-bag was carry-on sized (yeah, I was that good at my job, at prepping for unknown events ahead), and with a snort at my inner ego, I went to the rental counter to pick up a generic silver sedan that would take me into Campbell.

Well, to the hospital just inside Darlington's borders that served this area.

The Tri-Valleys was a cluster of three towns sandwiched between two mountain ranges, the fertile hills and valleys—there *was* a reason for the community's name after all—making for vast expanses of grazing areas for cattle, along with the odd bison and fields of wheat and barley.

It was small. It was close-knit.

It was painfully confining.

And I was back.

"Yay," I grumbled, navigating out of the airport's loop and heading east, toward the borders of Wyoming and Colorado, where the ground turned less desert and more tree-filled, over the small mountains that dropped me into the Tri-Valleys. Quiet, and like many small towns in middle America, fairly forgettable, with only the occasional blip in the news.

A high school team won the State Championship.

A local woman hit it big with a TV show on a food channel.

A drug bust made by a local officer.

Normal lives, knowing all the neighbors, main streets that were filled with only two lanes of traffic. A town who knew each other's schedules and routines, who baked casseroles and started meal trains after funerals or babies or illnesses.

They cared.

Of course, they also occasionally cared *too* much, were *too* nosy, always had an opinion and a judgment because they had plenty of time on their hands.

"Yeah, like Hollywood is any better?" I muttered to myself, navigating through the off-ramp, knowing in my heart of hearts it wasn't. People were just as nosy, just as judgmental. They just had more money, had bigger egos, and generally didn't show up on my front porch with a homemade casserole in hand.

I turned right, taking the road that would lead me to the county hospital, and frowned when I had to squint slightly. Tucked into the valley and with the setting sun behind me, it was getting dark fast.

I slipped off my sunglasses as I navigated the winding road, wishing I'd left my contacts in because the switch from prescription sunglasses to regular prescription glasses while driving was never easy, but it was levels of difficulty higher when it was someone as blind as me doing the change. My eyes had been aching from the dry airplane air and had needed a rest, so I'd made the swap from my usual contacts to glasses, and then the sun had been blinding until I'd turned off the highway.

Now it was dark, and I was using an elbow, a knee, and one hand to drive, the other fumbling to retrieve my glasses holder from my purse, open it, and get them on my face. I should have just pulled over to the side of the road.

But I hadn't.

And anyway, while these roads were winding, they were also empty. A shortcut locals took to bypass the often congested stretch of highway—

"Shit!"

I swerved as I navigated a corner, my glasses settling on my nose just as a truck came around the bend, going the opposite direction.

Their horn blared.

Deserved, I knew, since I'd been crowding the center line.

I waved, wrinkled my nose to slide my glasses firmly in place, and put both hands back on the wheel.

"No more shenanigans, Allen," I said. "It's shameful to the family name."

The scold was murmured aloud, but it echoed in my brain, drifting through in my dad's voice, bringing two things.

Guilt.

Awareness.

Guilt for leaving. Guilt because he was in the hospital. Guilt that he was alone.

Awareness . . . that there was a truck following very closely behind me.

Quite possibly, or perhaps, quite *likely*, the same truck who'd just honked at me.

Fear chased awareness down my spine, those headlights shining more brightly as the sun went down in my rearview, the bumper very close to mine, the large silhouette obvious when I glanced behind me.

Male. Big.

But I couldn't make out his face, and when I went to pull over on the shoulder, to slide to the side to let him pass, the truck just slowed behind me.

"Shit," I whispered, maneuvering back onto the road.

What should I do?

Drive to the police station? To the hospital like I'd planned? To the center of town and hope that even though the sun had now set, there would still be a few people around and this guy wouldn't turn ax murderer, just because I'd almost side-swiped him?

I mean, I *got* that I'd almost side-swiped him, but that was just it. Almost.

A horn. A middle finger. Move on.

Not follow me to town.

Which, thankfully, I could see up ahead, a few lights dotting the hills in the distance. A strip of them straight ahead, signaling the cute little downtown area, a gathering of bright lights to the right, highlighting the squat, modern hospital building.

Police station, hospital, or downtown?

My eyes flicked to the mirror, saw the truck was still behind me.

"Shit."

I didn't turn right to the hospital.

The sheriff's office was only a few streets down. Hopefully, whoever was behind me would see that I was heading that direction and get scared off.

But the closer I got to the station, the closer the truck seemed to get behind me.

Two more intersections.

One.

Then the sign for the Tri-Valleys Sheriff's Department came into view.

I breathed in a sigh of relief, turned right into the parking lot, and my anxiety calmed when I saw lights on in the lobby, people milling about.

A flash behind me.

I pulled up to the front of the building, grabbed my purse, and yanked at the handle, but the door opened before I could shove it wide.

My scream bubbled up in my throat—

"Don't."

Cold then hot. Terror dissolved to mist.

Aaron.

"What the fuck do you think you're doing?"

THREE

Aaron

I'D KNOWN it was her.

Even in the waning sunlight, even though I hadn't seen her in years, my body had reacted the same way it always did.

Pulse skipping.

Cock twitching.

Hands itching to touch.

Luckily, the physical response was easy to ignore.

Because I remembered the emotional crater she'd left behind with painful clarity. Fuck, but this woman had broken my heart.

"A-aaron?" she stammered, glancing up at me.

"Want to explain why you almost side-swiped me?"

Her chin lifted. "Want to explain why you tailgated me the entire way here? If I'd had to slam on my brakes—"

I stepped closer, some deep, hidden part of me I liked to imagine no longer existed revealed itself, exposing my yearning for her. For so long I'd pretended that need had just poofed off like smoke the moment she'd packed her car and disappeared into the sunset. It hadn't, and that secret piece deep inside reveled in seeing the fire in her eyes. In inhaling her scent, peaches and cream with a hint of cinnamon, spice she had inside and out.

Life.

She'd always been so full of it.

Even though now she was older, her body curvier, a sprinkle of lines just visible at the corners of her eyes. Her glasses hid them for the most part, but I knew her face better than my own, could easily catalog what had changed—

And what had stayed the same.

"You were changing your glasses," I said, taking another step toward her, until our bodies were only a hairsbreadth apart.

Her breath caught. But then the chin I'd cupped more than once, using it to tilt her head back, to get her mouth at the absolute perfect angle in order to kiss her, to taste her, to hold her, lifted.

"Move back," she snapped, shoving at my chest.

Then froze.

I froze.

Because the contact was a lightning rod.

And she seemed to feel the same way, yanking her hands back like they'd been burned, slipping to the side, and clutching her purse to her chest like it was a shield.

"You didn't answer me," he gritted out.

Her glare intensified. "You didn't ask a freaking question, Aaron Weaver," she snapped. "And I'm not obligated to answer it anyway, even if you did."

My lips twitched, but my smile was more snark than amusement, and I had to stifle a derisive chuckle because, "You never did think you were required to answer for anything, did you?"

Beautiful. Called my body like a siren's song. Lived her life for herself without giving a shit about anyone else.

In other words, still. The. Same.

Quiet.

Annoyed, mainly at myself for being entranced by this woman, if only for a few seconds, I forced myself to focus on the conversation. I should know better than to let myself remember, to dream, to wish things had been different between us. Mags had proven that she might be intoxicating, gorgeous, and equal parts fun and sweet, but she'd proven just as intensely that she was ephemeral.

That she couldn't be trusted with another person's heart.

A slice of something I once would have chalked up to pain slid through her eyes, yet just as I knew she wasn't back in town permanently, knew she'd leave as soon as she'd assured herself her father was fine, I also knew that though the pain might be there, it wasn't a pain that motivated.

She might have remorse for hurting someone, but she still did it anyway.

And *that* was the cool reminder I needed to shove the power of her down, to lock the memories away, to step back and cross my arms.

"How is he?" she asked.

"Why don't you head to the hospital and find out?"

"I was." Her lips pressed flat then relaxed. "At least until a big truck began tailgating my car and scared the daylights out of me."

The words and tone were tough, but fear was back in her eyes.

Not for herself, but for the one family member she had left.

Enough that I found the need to take it away.

"Warren's fine," I said, watching relief wash over her face. "His surgery went well, and he'd already taken a lap on that hip by the time I left. He'll be discharged tomorrow."

"So soon?"

I shrugged. "They want them up and moving as quickly as possible after these kinds of surgeries."

She nodded. "Right."

And silence. Uncomfortable, sticky, and hot despite the cold air and dirty piles of snow plowed to the sides of the parking lot. It pissed me off that she could affect me this way, that she still had a hold on some part of me, even when I'd thought anything tying us together was gone. I'd locked up the memories, burned them to ash with fury and disappointment, but this woman still had the power to get to me.

It was fucking infuriating.

"Why are you here?"

She jumped at my change in tone, but fuck if I would feel guilty about startling her, not after everything that had happened.

"I'm here for my dad."

"And when are you leaving?"

So I could count down the days until she left.

Not because, even after everything had gone down, part of me didn't want to see her go again.

She was quiet for a heartbeat then said, "I've cleared a week."

"Hop in, hop out," I muttered, furious but knowing it had little to do with her taking a week off work to come and care for her dad, knowing it had everything and nothing to do with me.

I had no clue if it was the everything or the nothing part that was bothering me.

Everything—a pathetic part of me wanted her to be here for a week to see me.

Nothing—the thought of her returning without wanting to see me hurt more than it should.

Which was not at all, of course.

Not that any of this mattered. Both scenarios were ice picks to the heart . . . and also enough to remind me of myself. Years had passed. I was a fully formed adult with a career that took me to many places outside of Campbell, outside of Utah, outside of the USA. My life was busy and hectic, and I was content.

Because I didn't let myself be wrapped up in women, and most especially not in women who were flighty and would be gone again before the week was out.

"That's not fair," she said.

"Life's not fair," I countered.

Her eyes narrowed. "I'll make arrangements to stay longer if I need to."

"Congratulations." I mimed, reaching into my pocket and pulling out a trophy. "Here's your Best Daughter in the Universe Award."

"I—"

"Stay your week," I said and spun in the direction of my truck. "I'm good at picking up the pieces when you leave."

FOUR

Maggie

HE LEFT in a cloud of exhaust, just as the front door of the police station opened.

"Everything okay?" a female deputy asked, blond hair slicked back into a ponytail, gaze fixing me in place.

"Fine," I said. "We just had a close call on the road, and he wanted to make sure I was o—" I gasped. "Tammy, oh my God! Is that you?"

"Yes—*Maggie?* Holy shit! I haven't seen you in years."

I rounded the hood of my car, a huge smile breaking out on my face as I closed the distance to one of the few people I'd been close to in high school. We hugged, and I pulled back. "You're here in Campbell," I exclaimed. "How? Why? I—"

"Me?" she said. "How about *you?* I've been back for two years now. You're the one who hit the road and didn't look back."

"I've visited my dad a few times," I told her. "But yeah, I've been a little busy."

A smirk. "Working for Pierce Daniels?" She nudged my

shoulder. "Please, tell me he's as nice in real life as he pretends to be in interviews."

"He is," I said then stage whispered, "and don't tell him, but Artie is actually my favorite."

Tammy grinned. "Is she as great as she seems, too?"

"She's awesome." I thought of the first client who'd given me a really great opportunity. Not to just be a person to organize her hair and nail appointments, to pick up her food or dry cleaning—though I'd cut my teeth in the industry doing plenty of that—but to be involved in building something, a brand that I loved and was so damned proud to have been part of crafting.

And she'd led me to Pierce, to Eden, to Talbot.

I'd become a brand builder.

The brand builder.

Which sounded ridiculous outside of L.A., when the cold bite of air was in my nose, fogging my breath, when the first few snowfalls were piled on the sides of the parking lot.

Probably, there'd be a warm snap and the snow would be gone in a week, but it was here now, and a clear reminder of the difference between my current home and my former.

"You okay?"

"Yeah," I said. "I want to catch up more, but my dad—"

"Oh, shit." Tammy's eyes went wide. "Your dad. I'm sorry, I wasn't thinking. How is he?"

I shook my head. "Fine, I think. I just need to head to the hospital."

"Of course." She stepped back. "Still know how to drive in the snow?" she asked lightly, her gaze drifting from me to the parking lot.

"I made it this far, didn't I?"

Tammy chuckled. "Not sure if that's vouching for your driving skills."

"I've gotten better."

"Six mailboxes from our teenage years and the driver of the truck that was just in here would speak differently."

"That was Aaron."

"Ah." Knowing invaded her expression.

"It's not like that."

"Not sure it ever has been or will ever be *not like that.*"

I sighed but didn't agree with her. Mostly because I was mature enough to know she was right. Aaron and I had always been drawn to each other, and though hurting him by leaving, by breaking things off when he'd wanted to get serious, was one of my biggest regrets, I still wouldn't change anything.

I'd needed to go.

We were too young. Too unformed. Too—

Wrapped up in each other to become separate people.

We wouldn't have lasted.

I just cut the cord before we would have imploded.

Tammy squeezed my arm, handed me a card. "My cell is on there. Let's grab a meal later in the week, when things are calmer on your end."

"I'd like that."

We said our goodbyes, I got back into my rental, and I navigated my way to the hospital, this time without any near misses, this time not almost side-swiping any big trucks, this time alone.

Just me and the open road.

Exactly as I preferred.

THE OPEN ROAD was short this time around.

Just a ten-minute drive to a hospital I'd visited enough that I knew where to park, knew how to find the information desk, knew where the pediatricians were when my dad had taken me for my yearly checkup, where the gynecologists were when I'd made my own secret appointment in order to get birth control—because this was a small town and Aaron and I had been together for a long time. I'd loved him, but if I wasn't ready to be engaged, and for the subsequent big wedding, then I definitely wasn't ready for an accidental pregnancy.

Birth control pills *and* condoms.

Because safety first.

God, I'd been a stubborn thing back then. Not that demanding we use protection was a bad thing, not by a long shot, but I'd . . . just seen the world in such simple terms. Black and white, no gray zones.

I had enough years on me now to know that the world was nearly all gray.

Things were rarely clear cut, rarely simple or easy or obvious.

Of course, I was also still on the pill, still made my partners wear condoms, so even though I'd learned and grown as a person, some things never changed. Especially the important ones.

Like Aaron.

Gorgeous, steadfast Aaron.

Blinking that thought away, I ignored the hallways off to the sides that would lead to the pediatric and OB-GYN departments and approached the information desk smack dab in the middle of the rotunda.

"I'm here to see my father," I told the older woman in pale purple scrubs. "Warren Allen. He had hip surgery earlier today."

"Can I see some identification?"

I pulled out my license, handed it over to be scrutinized for a few moments before she typed a few things into the computer in front of her. "Fourth floor," she said, looking up and passing my ID back. "A Wing. Room 492. Just take the elevators there," she added, pointing behind her.

"Thank you."

A few moments later, I was on the metal deathtrap—okay, so I wasn't a big fan of small, enclosed spaces, but I liked the idea of heading up four flights of stairs on tired ass legs even less. Anyway, it was faster to just take the elevator, and I wasn't so terrified of them that I couldn't ride.

Before I could really freak out about the fact that I was hanging over a pit by just one cable—yes, I knew all about emergency brakes and backup cables, but logic didn't always reign with fear, did it?—*anyway*, before I got really panicked the steel doors opened and I stepped off, following the signs to the A Wing. I checked in at the nurse's station then followed several more signs until I got to room 492.

A quick knock before I poked my head inside.

One bed, some monitors, a dimmed set of overhead lights and . . . my dad.

My heart seized.

It had been just under six months since I'd visited for his birthday weekend, bringing with me a screener for Artie's latest film.

I'd been listed as a producer.

Assistant. Publicist. Now producer.

A side gig, because I definitely preferred the PR side, but it was still fun to experiment and have my voice heard, especially on a cool project shot by women, made for women, and written by women.

And one that had been the biggest box office success of the year.

Fucking big time.

Big enough that my dad's smile had been huge, larger than I'd ever seen.

Proud. His flighty daughter, who never made a decision he approved of, had her name in the credits of a huge Hollywood film. So, while he might not understand what I did with branding and creating a public image, how I finessed a social media presence, he did understand end credits and a white name blazed across a black background.

For once, I'd made him proud.

Now he was in the hospital, eyes closed, mouth slightly parted in sleep, body looking way too small and frail in the bed, and for the first time in my adult life, I was critically aware that my father was getting older.

I made my way across the room on quiet feet and slid into the chair next to the bed, reaching over the rail and wrapping my hand around his.

He stirred, lids starting to slide open.

"Shh," I told him. "Sleep. It's okay."

My words had the opposite effect. His eyes flew open. "Mags?"

I smiled, squeezed his hand lightly. "Yeah, Dad. It's me."

Sleep disappeared as a frown pulled down his brows. "Why?"

"What?"

"Why are you here?" Disappointment laced his question and pain sliced through me, hot and sharp, so fucking reminiscent of my childhood that I actually felt my lungs freeze. Damn. I loved my dad so much. He was my family. My only tie to my mother, to my past, to my history.

But he could cut me to the quick more efficiently than any other person on the planet.

I inhaled, kept the hurt out of my response. "Because you're in the hospital."

It was instinctive, to hide that pain. I'd done it so often over the years that it was easy. Unremarkable.

He wasn't an easy man to love. He'd influenced my black-and-white version of the world very heavily. His opinions were weighted with the experience of his past—a woman who'd gone and died on him (his words) and a daughter who was headstrong to the extreme (also his words).

For a long time I'd thought that part of me—the piece that infuriated and perplexed him in equal measures—came from my mother.

Now, I knew that though that might be true in some ways, it wasn't true in any way that mattered. My stubbornness and persistence came from him. My work ethic came from him. My tunnel vision and ability to only truly acknowledge what I gleaned as the right course of action came from *him*.

Thankfully, I'd grown out of the final two for the most part.

But as was typical of people my age, I considered myself a work in progress. Past the blush of arrogance and know-it-all-ness of my early twenties, though not yet slipping into the rigor and opinions in stasis that sometimes came later in life.

I was very aware of my faults.

Some I wore like badges of honor.

Others I attempted to change . . . with varying degrees of success.

And sometimes they weren't able to be changed at all. Like staring at my father's face, seeing him displeased—again—and feeling like a naughty child *again*.

"I'm fine," he muttered, turning his head to the side, eyes slamming shut, tugging his fingers from mine.

"What happened?" I asked carefully, tucking my hands into my lap. "The management company got their payment this month, everything on the outside of the house should be taken care of, even snow."

Silence.

"Dad," I tried again. "I know I'm not close, but I've been

trying to make sure you're cared for. You shouldn't be shoveling with your heart—"

"My goddamned heart is fine," he snapped, still not looking at me. "Just go."

"What?"

"Go. *G. O.* Leave me in peace."

"I took time off work to come to see you," I said, still careful, but this time it was careful to not let the hurt bleed into my tone. "I was worried when I found out you'd fallen."

"And I'll be having words with Aaron for that," my dad snapped. "It's none of your business—"

"You're my dad. How is it not my business?"

Mulish.

His expression had gone mulish. His jaw tight. His lips pressed flat. I knew there was no point in pressing this, knew I'd get nowhere except for an aching head and a throbbing heart.

But I'd gotten my stubborn from him.

So, I pushed.

"How is it not my business?" I asked again.

A tense pause. Then, "You made it that way."

Breath slicing out, stinging my throat on its exit. Or maybe that was the burn of tears I fought to hold back. "I've been home for your birthday. For Christmas. I was here to see you through the recovery of four heart attacks." To the detriment of my career at that point, as I'd had to quit my assistant duties at the time. Although I'd gotten back on track, I'd always made my dad a priority, even when he hadn't done the same for me. "It's why I pay thousands of dollars a month for the company to take care of the ranch, to shovel snow, and stock your fridge and freezer so you can concentrate on the stuff you love."

It was why I hadn't been able to afford a house yet, why I still rented out a guest house on Artie and Pierce's L.A. property, even though my salaries from them and Talbot and Eden were very generous.

The rent paid was at my insistence and against Artie and Pierce's wishes, since they'd offered the space for free.

But I'd always made my own way, and that wasn't going to stop now.

"I didn't ask you to do that."

A sigh slipped through my lips. "I know. I *want* to take care of you. I want you to move out to California so we can be closer, but I know you're happy here," I told him. "Which means I want you to be able to stay here safely."

"I'm not a fucking child!"

I sat back, the force of the loud outburst shocking after the quiet argument of the previous minutes.

The same old pattern.

Why was I surprised?

Push, push, explode.

A deep, deep breath. Old pain shoved down. Calm words grasped onto by the tips of my fingernails.

"I didn't say you were."

His chest rose and fell in rapid gusts, the *beep-beep, beep-beep* of his pulse pinging through the speakers of the monitors.

"Do you want me to go?"

"Yes."

No hesitation. No delay. Just one sharp syllable, and I was again wondering why I kept doing this. Why I continued trying to make something full and rich and . . . warm with my father when it wouldn't be.

Oh, I thought he loved me in his own way.

But that was rough with barbed edges and wholly dependent on me following the rules he set out and believed made for a full life.

I didn't want that.

Never had. Never would.

Thus, the crux of our dissent—one that would never be fixed.

Two stubborn Allens, each a separate planet in their own orbit who would never collide. Never connect.

I pushed to my feet. "Goodnight, Dad." I headed for the door.

"*Good* riddance." A soft utterance, but one that still reached my ears.

One that sliced and stabbed, even though I wanted to be impervious. I reached for the handle, tugged the door open.

"I love you."

I didn't wait for a reply.

Because I knew one wouldn't come anyway.

FIVE

Aaron

I HEARD the gravel before I saw the lights.

Much later than I expected, given that visiting hours had been over more than four hours earlier, and also based on the knowledge that Warren and Maggie together were oil and water.

Five minutes. Ten tops until they were at each other's throats.

Until Maggie stormed off, hurt masked by anger.

Predictable as a summer heat wave, as my body's attraction to hers.

A flash of light shining through the thin panel of curtains that adorned the windows in the bunkhouse. They weren't designed to keep out illumination, the ranch hands needing to rise with the sun.

But the bunkhouse wasn't used for temporary workers—here for the summer and helping with the cattle—any longer.

Hills empty of cows, no hay bales to disperse in the winter or troughs to check and ensure the water inside wasn't frozen through. The ranch was quiet, a soft and peaceful expanse of peaks and valleys that had been earned by a man's hard work.

To the detriment of many other things.

I got that now.

Still liked the tough old bastard, but I knew he hadn't made things easy on Maggie, just as I knew it had factored into her decision to leave and to stay away.

It wasn't fair to put the blame solely on her. Or Warren, for that matter.

Not when I'd had my own part in motivating Maggie's flight.

The understanding that came with adulthood was a heavy thing. But it still didn't erase the past. Didn't make what she'd done okay. Maybe I got why she'd felt it necessary to go, but—

She'd left without me.

Of course, she'd also asked me to go with her before school had gotten out for the summer—

"Fuck," I said.

I couldn't have gone. Just uproot my life and—

"*Fuck*," I said again, the swirling of thoughts that had kept me up for the last hours quieting with the realization that the lights hadn't moved. They shone through my window, illuminating the nearly empty space as her car idled outside.

I sat up, pushed out of bed, and went to the door. Mags was parked in front of the bunkhouse, the engine running in her rental, headlights shining bright, her profile silhouetted through the car's passenger side window. Or part of her profile anyway. She had her forehead resting against the steering wheel, hands fisted around it.

And she wasn't moving.

Fuck.

This time I only said it in my head.

I still stepped back into the bunkhouse, shoved my feet into my boots, and walked toward her car anyway. Gravel crunched, the engine growled, the quiet of the night fully broken. But the disturbance of peace wasn't why I kept walking.

Moth to a flame.

That was me.

I rounded the hood, heading toward her door, and paused, waiting to see if she'd feel me standing there.

If the invisible thread tying us together was still in place for her, too.

I found it was.

The moment I stopped walking, she lifted her head, neck swiveling until her eyes met mine.

Heat.

Desire.

Fury.

All flooded my gut, my heart, my mind, even as I stared into her eyes and saw . . . nothing.

She was blank.

I knew that look, and it had me reaching for the door handle, hauling it open, knowing exactly what caused it.

She didn't move or turn away as I reached for the keys, as I rotated them and turned off the engine. Hot breath on my cheek, peaches and spice in my nose. I inhaled, pulling her scent deep into my lungs then clenching my jaw against the furious need to shift closer, to press my nose to her throat, to nuzzle in, and let her smell wash over me.

Her fingers would come to my hair, nails biting at my scalp, encouraging me closer, until her mouth found mine.

I snaked a hand out, pressed the latch on her seat belt, and retreated.

She was leaving. She might be luscious and prettier as an almost thirty-year-old woman, but . . . she couldn't be trusted.

Maggie released a shuddering breath that told me enough.

The tie was absolutely still there.

The troubled glance those brown eyes sent my way said she knew it was, too, and that she understood, just like me, the link that was still present was dangerous for us both.

She shifted, turning in her seat to retrieve a small duffle bag from behind the passenger seat. "Aaron," she said, tone empty, even as those eyes remained troubled.

"Mags."

She pushed out of the car, slammed the door. "Why are you here?"

I studied her face, the way her gaze never quite met mine. "I'm living in the bunkhouse." Had been living there on and off for years, staying any time I was in town. In the beginning because I'd felt some obligation to watch out for whatever fragile connections I had left with Maggie's dad, and I'd pitched in as necessary on the ranch. Later, as my wine business grew, as I became more restless to figure out my place in the world. France? California? Italy? None had quite fit, and inevitably I always came home looking for . . . connection. Or maybe it was a shared experience. Warren had nearly been my father-in-law, he'd experienced the same loss. He understood the hole Maggie left.

He knew how furious it could make a man.

We could commiserate together.

We could turn into ornery bastards together.

Or maybe that was just me.

"I—" A shake of her head. "You're living in the bunkhouse?"

I shrugged.

"For how long?"

Another shrug. "A while."

Her eyes flitted to mine, away. "And when I come to visit?"

"It's twice a year, Mags," I told her. "Not that hard to make sure we're not here at the same time. Not that hard to get out of town."

"Get out of—" She shouldered her bag, hurt drifting across her expression before it was carefully tucked away. "Never mind. I-I'm going to bed. I'll be out of your hair in the morning, so don't worry about getting out of town to get away from me. I'll save you the trouble."

"You're good at leaving."

Chin lifting, shoulders straightening . . . numb was back.

Only this time it was from me, not her dad.

I tried to ignore how that made me feel, opened my mouth to tell her—

"You're right," she said quietly. "Good night." She bleeped the locks on the car, a habit she must have picked up in California because no one locked their doors in Campbell, Utah—car, tractor, house, or otherwise.

"Mags," I said when she'd reached the bottom step.

She stopped but didn't turn around.

"It's because he missed you."

Not the words I'd intended to say, the ones reminding her that the power in the kitchen could be finicky and to reset the breaker if there was an issue with the toaster in the morning.

Instead, I'd said *that*.

Instead, I'd said something where I didn't know if the *he* I was referring to was me or her dad.

I held my breath, watching as she stood statue-still for several long seconds. Then she unstuck, walked up the three steps leading to the front door, and pushed inside. The wooden panel closed behind her, another *snick* telling me her locking habits had extended to front doors as well.

A light in the hall flicked on.

Then off.

Another turned on in her old bedroom. Stayed on.

I should have gone to bed, crunched my way over to the bunkhouse and gone to bed.

Instead, I waited until the light finally went off.

Only then did I head back inside and try to go to sleep.

Try being the operative word.

Because every time I closed my eyes, I could see the blank expression that had slid into place at my admission.

Numb. From me.

It shouldn't matter.

It did . . . and I hated myself because of it.

I STUMBLED across the gravel toward the main house, eyes blurry, bare feet in my boots, mind desperately needing a cup of coffee.

The sun was way too bright, even though I'd missed my normal wakeup time by several hours because of my inability to sleep the night before. I had a shit-ton of emails to hit, then the hospital to get to. Warren would be anxious to get home, and the doctor who'd seen him had said he could come home early afternoon.

I needed to make sure he had food, that his bed was clean, and nothing was around that he'd trip over, especially in his more fragile state.

Reaching for the doorknob and smiling because I knew exactly what he would think of being described as fragile, even if it was just a temporary state, I stopped and stared dumbly at the hunk of metal when it didn't shift in my hand.

I twisted it again.

It didn't move.

More staring. More foggy brain trying to process why the

knob wasn't turning before I remembered Maggie and her newfound habit of locking things.

Stifling a groan, I shuffled my way over to the pot of dying flowers in one corner, the arrangement having been bright and colorful six months before when Maggie had planted it but was now a collection of crispy and dry leaves and broken petals because Warren hadn't bothered to water it.

I sighed, knowing there was way too much to unpack there for my uncaffeinated brain, and kicked the pot to the side, revealing the spare key underneath.

Into the lock, hearing and feeling the *click* as it disengaged.

Pushing into the entry, stumbling to the kitchen, opening a cabinet to grab the coffee grounds, and—

Finding it empty.

What in the actual fuck?

I blinked, frowned at the perfectly-coffee-bag-sized hole in the line of food. Pancake mix, sugar, greasing spray, salt and pepper, missing coffee bag, a tidy row of spices that I knew for a fact Warren didn't use.

But no coffee.

"Looking for this?"

I swiveled to the side, saw Mags leaning against the counter, the bag of coffee in her hand. I watched as she filled the pot to brew, replaced the carafe, and started the machine.

A hiss.

A bubble.

The rich smell of caffeine hitting my nose.

One inhale, and I was well on my way to being alert. Or, at least more human and less zombie.

"You're still the same in the morning," she said softly.

I'd been contemplating making myself a piece of toast. The company that Mags had hired to look out for the place included a Larry.

Larry could shovel snow—when he didn't throw out his back and rely on his teenage son to complete the task. A fact that I'd discovered the previous day when Larry had heard the news of what had happened to Warren and had hobbled his way into the waiting room, beyond guilty and pissed at his son.

Who was bound for some serious grounding, I figured.

But I'd been a teenager many moons before. I got it. Sometimes teenagers were idiots and didn't think stuff through. Larry's son clearly hadn't expected Warren, post four heart attacks and on increasingly shaky feet, to undertake a huge shoveling job.

The concrete was new.

That was what Warren had told me anyway, a dip into his savings with a concrete driveway planned for the spring.

I thought it was smart. Easier for Warren to get in and out, better for any deliveries or visitors to not have to navigate the gravel, and inevitably as time went on, the mud.

I had not anticipated that Warren would think it necessary to not have his concrete "ruined" by the snowfall, whatever that meant. So, instead of shoveling the walk like I'd considered before dismissing the idea because the grounds team always came on Friday afternoons, I'd gone to town to meet with a new client. And Larry hadn't come.

Larry's *son* hadn't come.

And Warren had decided to shovel the walk.

A freak fucking snowstorm that week had led to me coming back to the ranch to find him sprawled on the "new" concrete, leg twisted in a direction it shouldn't be, and his lips a scary shade of purple.

Now Maggie was back.

Mags who was interrupting my contemplation of Larry and all his skills, which also included bread making and canning.

Delicious sourdough. Peach preserves.

I was fantasizing about that almost as much as the coffee. Or maybe, the lack of caffeine was making my mind malfunction.

It wouldn't be the first time.

Unfortunately, I didn't think the malfunction was stimulant-related . . . hell, it was *most definitely* stimulant-related, just of the heart and cock variety rather than the caffeinated version.

"Drink." A mug appeared in front of my nose.

My fingers had grasped it, bringing it to my lips before I even processed the movement. Then delicious black coffee was hitting my tongue. Like the scent wafting up to my nose, the taste alone helped me shake off the remnants of sleep.

I wasn't totally awake, but I was pretty damned close.

Finishing the rest of my mug in a few big gulps, I finally took in the sight of the kitchen.

Maggie was wearing a pair of sweats and a baggy T-shirt, her feet in socks, her long black hair pulled into a ponytail that was less about containment and more about loosely holding back her locks from her face as they scattered this way and that over her nape. But it was the countertops that had thrown me for a loop, perhaps even more than my brain before coffee.

Okay, not *that* bad.

But I definitely wasn't prepared for there to be multiple foil-wrapped packages lined up on the counters.

"Is that—?" I shook myself, forgot about sourdough and peach preserves. "Is that cinnamon apple bread?"

The barest ghost of a smile on the counter. "For you? Yes." She began loading the loaves into a bag. "But you have to promise to stow them in the bunkhouse, since Dad can't eat them on his diet."

I set my mug down in a hurry when she extended the bag toward me. "I promise," I said, mouth already salivating in memory of the deliciousness that awaited. This was, hands down, my favorite thing she'd ever cooked. And considering she'd grown up with a father who could sear the deliciousness out of anything from vegetables to meat to pancakes, she'd started practicing early. She'd gotten good, but the best thing she'd created was cinnamon apple bread. "But you know he'll sniff it out."

A chuckle, but reserved, unlike her laughter from before she'd left home. "I made a low-fat variety." She nodded at the loaves on the opposite counter. "Yours will be safe," she added when I must have made the skepticism in my mind clear on my face. "You can't taste the difference, I swear."

My Spidey senses tingled. "Why not just make them all that way?"

She shrugged. "I didn't have enough ingredients to make two batches."

Hmm.

Plausible, but something was telling me that wasn't the whole story. I turned, refilled my mug as I pondered that. Something in her tone was off, but Mags was stubborn, and direct contact never served to get me the answers I wanted.

She began gathering the other loaves, stowing some in the freezer, putting a couple in a different bag, leaving one on the counter before wiping down the tiles and starting in on the dishes. "I'm going to get dressed, drop these off with Tammy at the station. Then I'll get Dad home, check in with Larry and make sure this doesn't happen again—"

"Larry threw his back out."

Mag's lips parted. "Oh no."

"His son was supposed to clear the walk, but he didn't come."

A nod. "Right. Well, I'll talk to Larry and make sure he knows to contact the agency to cover any gaps rather than relying on the minimal sense that a teenage boy possesses."

I grinned, in complete agreement with her on that. "Okay."

Another nod. "Right. So, I'll make sure Dad is settled and take off, get out of his and your hair." She went to the cabinet, grabbed a mug out, and I frowned.

"You drink coffee now?"

Mags made a face. "Still can't stand the stuff." She nodded at a kettle I knew was only used when she was in town because Warren sure as hell didn't have any desire for a drink that wasn't coffee or beer. "Tea for me."

"You didn't use to like even that."

"I gave up diet soda."

I leaned back against the counter, crossed my arms. "I don't believe it."

She ignored me, pulling a tea bag out from somewhere before filling the mug with hot water, and picking it up. "I'm going to get ready. If I don't see you again"—her eyes lifted but didn't meet mine, and I knew it was a deliberate omission —"thanks for your help. I've got the rugs picked up, his sheets changed. All the outstanding laundry done, and I've got the same nurse, Claudette, who took care of him after his heart attacks, coming this afternoon. She'll be here for a week, so Dad will be—"

"You're really going?" I asked.

Her gaze was on the mug, fingers wrapped around the string as she waited for the tea to steep. "I don't think there's a point in me staying," she eventually said. "I'll do my duty as I always do, but I won't stay here and make him miserable."

"You don't—"

"Think before you finish that statement, Aaron," she interrupted. "Only now, I get the unique joy of making *both* you and him miserable."

"And yet you made cinnamon apple bread."

"I couldn't sleep." She picked up her mug, turned for the hall.

"Full-fat *and* low-fat."

Mags snorted. "Is that the barometer of a loving daughter now? Low-fat cinnamon apple bread."

It sure as hell wasn't the barometer of someone who was completely detached.

"And anyway," she went on. "You don't want me here. I get it. I'll take care of the final details and head to the hotel tonight."

My brows drew down. "Hotel?"

"First flight out in the morning is at five," she said. "It's easier if I just stay near the airport."

"Easier for who?" I asked, even as I wondered why in the fuck I was pushing this. She wanted to leave, great. She could go, the proverbial door hitting her on the ass on the way out. But numb eyes, shadows beneath those unfathomable pools of a deep, rich brown, and . . . cinnamon apple bread.

Separate batches.

For two men in her life who held on to no little amount of anger about her choices.

Separate batches. Numb. Shadows.

My heart constricted.

"Easier for him. For you," she said, tone filling with granite. "For me."

I took the mug from her hands, not having realized that I'd closed the distance between us until my fingers were on the warm porcelain, until I was searching her eyes for the flecks of gray that only someone who was this close—inches separating us—could see. Steel in warmth. Determination peeking through soft.

"Why did you make separate batches?" I asked.

She took a step back. "I told you—"

"No, Mags," I said, halting her with a hand on her arm. "The truth."

Her jaw tightened. "I don't—"

I brushed my thumb along the tight muscles ticking there, my pulse speeding up at the feel of her skin beneath mine, sparks shooting down my fingers, my arm. One touch that reminded me so intensely of everything that had come before. One touch that made me forget all of what had come after. "Why, Peaches?"

Her lips parted on a shuddering exhale. "Don't," she murmured.

I stroked my thumb again, reveling in the sparks. "Why?"

Eyes slid closed, her body drifted the slightest bit forward. "I hate that I hurt you, and I thought if I made—" Her words cut off, probably because I'd stiffened. Lids peeling back. "I hurt you, and I'm sorry. I can't make that right. I just thought—"

I retreated a step, pulse pounding for a different reason this time. "You just thought you could make some dumb ass recipe from a decade ago, and I'd magically forgive you for running?" Ignoring the voice that said I'd forgiven her a long time ago for leaving town, that the only reason I was angry now was because I was furious that I'd wasted so much time and energy hating her, I turned and strode to the sink, dumping the coffee and washing the mug with more vigor than was necessary.

"That's not—" she began. "I couldn't sleep, and I was thinking about the good times."

"Good times," I spat, not liking this side of me, but unable to stop it from bursting free.

"I am sorry I hurt you," she said and sighed. "But I'm not sorry I left. Did I want you to find the courage to come with me? Hell *yes*, I did. But do I also think we would have ended up in a place very much like this?" She set her cup on the counter with a quiet *clink*. "With you pissed that I couldn't be the person you wanted me to be? How can I think anything different? We were too young, in a relationship that was too serious, and with two wildly different ideas of what we wanted for the future."

I spun back to face her. "We could have made it work."

A sad shake of her head. "No, Aaron, we couldn't have. Either you would have had to sacrifice want you wanted, or I would have had to. Eventually, one of us would have become resentful, and we would have imploded." Her mouth pressed flat, eyes no longer numb, instead rubbed dull by the painful memories. "Did it hurt like hell when you told me you wouldn't come? Of course, it did. Did it hurt worse to leave you, anyway? Yes, so much so that I almost forgot it all and turned back anyway."

Yeah, sure. Except, she hadn't. She'd had plenty of time to reconsider. A decade's worth. "But you didn't."

"You think it was hard being here?" she asked. "You had *everything.* You had everyone around you, loving on you, treating you like you were the one who was wronged, or at least the only one who was hurt."

"You could have had that, too," I pointed out.

"I could have stayed. You could have come." She threw up her hands, paced a few feet away before turning back. "It doesn't matter now, though, does it? Life moves on." A sigh as she came close again. "But Aaron, until you realize how unfair it was for you to put that pressure on me to give up my dream, knowing that for *years* all I'd ever wanted was to move to L.A., to work in films, you'll never truly understand why I *had* to go."

No. I got that already. I knew I was wrong to have pushed her to—

Her arm lifted as though she was going to stroke my cheek. "And when I heard your mom was sick—"

"Don't." Fury roared to life at the mention of my mother. God, I'd been heartbroken, totally devasted from Maggie leaving, and then we'd had a family meeting, and I'd been terrified I would lose my mom, too.

"Aaron—"

I stepped to the side, grabbed the bag of cinnamon apple bread, and dropped it into the trash, furious that I was affected by this woman again. I should be over it, over her, over a dumb ass high-school-aged broken heart.

And how can you do that when you live with her father for half the year?

Something my mom had said repeatedly in the years since, nearly a decade in remission, but a looming reality that terrified me whenever she went for her yearly checkup.

You're traumatized because you lost Maggie and then you nearly lost me, and now you're grasping at the straws of a life in the past, instead of living for the future.

Unfortunately, I was realizing that was also the truth.

One that was easier to ignore, easier to be pissed at Maggie for leaving in the first place.

Ironically, the final push for Mags to leave at all was me wanting to get married and start a family. So young. So stupid. But she'd gone, freeing me up to find that with another woman, but here I was, a decade later, single, a handful of relationships with potential in my past, a potential that had never bloomed . . .

Because she'd left, and something had broken in me.

"Fuck," I snapped, brushing past her and heading for the front door. "Do what you want, Mags. Leave like you're good at. Or stay and tough it out for a change. Try to bake your way into your father's heart." I paused, saw she'd trailed me, was watching me from the doorway of the kitchen. "But keep me out of it."

The numb crept back in even as she nodded, her voice even when she added, "I'll leave you out of it."

"Good." I shoved through the door, hauled ass across the gravel to the bunkhouse, grabbing clothes and heading into the shower.

By the time I was finished, the house was quiet, and her car was gone.

But when I stepped out of the bunkhouse, I had to do a quick side-step to avoid crushing the bag of cinnamon apple loaves I'd thrown in the trash. A note was stapled to the front.

I arranged for an earlier flight. Claudette will pick Dad up from the hospital since I know he'd prefer that anyway.

-M

P.S. No sense in this going to waste.

P.P.S. I am truly sorry I hurt you. But I never forgot what we had, and . . . I missed you more than you can know.

A SILVER CIRCLE was taped below the last, and it took me a minute to recognize it as the bracelet I'd scrimped and saved to buy for her senior year. The delicate shining chain held a single charm, a perfectly round peach with the tiniest fleck of a diamond at its stem.

Peaches.

Sweet with bite, a tough, rock-hard pit buried deep inside, an easily bruised outer fruit.

I'd forgotten *that*.

Not about peaches. About Maggie.

And now I had to wonder what else I would have remembered if I hadn't walked out of that kitchen, if I hadn't left.

I had to wonder if she was right.

Maybe it wasn't leaving so much as *staying* gone that was harder. Maybe even harder than being the one left behind.

I glanced down at the loaves, their delicious scent tempting and filling me with a longing that would never be assuaged.

Or maybe not.

Maybe being left was just as bad.

SIX

Maggie

THE PLANE BUMPED DOWN onto the runway, a smooth landing into LAX and hopefully a sign of things to come.

Taxiing, pulling into the gate, the doors disarmed, and then I was out of my seat, my go-bag once again tossed over my shoulder, a blast of warm air—at least compared to Utah—hitting me as I exited.

Bypassing baggage claim.

Out of the airport and to long-term parking.

Then into my car, the long drive through rush-hour traffic back to my place. Hitting the code on the gate, pulling into my spot in the covered carport next to the guest house, trying to quietly slip by the pool when I heard voices on the other side of the hedge.

Failing to go unnoticed.

"Mags?" Pierce called. "I thought you'd be gone a week."

I inhaled, held the air in my lungs long enough to steady my voice. Then I released it and said, "Plans changed."

There. Even and calm.

No one would notice a thing.

"I'll catch up with you later," I said, shifting my bag and moving toward the front door.

No response trailed me, and I thought I'd escaped, but then Artie appeared in the break in the hedge, the little gate that enclosed the pool closed, their daughter perched on her hip. Artie was beautiful, a surfer girl in looks, a killer business-woman in brains. A former child star only recently returned to the screen, she'd used her time away to grow her production company into one of the best in the industry.

Smart, gorgeous, nice.

And didn't miss a thing.

Which meant it took her precisely one look at my face to know that Utah had been a disaster.

She passed Brenna off to Pierce, pushed through the gate, and came over to grab my hands. "Mags, is . . . I mean . . . did something happen to your dad?"

I forced a smile. I should have realized she would be worried, thinking things had escalated from a relatively simple broken hip. "He's fine. Out of the hospital now. Things were"—a slow, even breath—"well, it was better for everyone that I come back."

Artie's fingers squeezed. "I'm sorry." A beat. "Want to talk about it?"

That was a hard no, which my boss and friend easily read. "Some other time," she said. "We'll have cocktails and kick Pierce out of the house and can self-medicate with pasta from The Restaurant."

The Restaurant being an eatery Artie was a silent partner in. One that had some of the best food I'd ever eaten.

"I thought they didn't do takeout."

She winked. "Sometimes it pays off to be the big boss."

I snorted. "Sounds good." I tilted my head, considering her

schedule. "How's Thursday? You just have that script meeting in the morning, but your evening is free, and you have nothing on Friday."

"Maggie Allen," Artie exclaimed, slipping her hands free to plunk them down onto her hips. "You are no longer in charge of my schedule," she reminded me. "I have another assistant for that because you've got your own schedule and clients now."

I rose on tiptoe, pressed a kiss to her cheek. "Old habits die hard."

She gave me a quick hug. "I know, babe." A pause. "You sure you don't want to talk?"

I felt flayed open, my heart and the pain I'd buried inside it exposed to the world. "Yeah. I just need some time."

"Understood." She stepped back. "Come over for dinner later if you're up for it. Otherwise, I'll talk to you soon and see you Thursday."

"Thanks, Artie."

"Love you, babe."

"I love you, too," I managed to say, meaning it, knowing she meant it, too, that it wasn't one of those Hollywood things where everyone *loved* everyone. Artemis had become family, more than my own.

And that made everything hurt all over again.

I raised a hand, turned away, and hurried to the door to the guest house reeling from the impact of her words, of the bond we'd built over the last few years—simple and strong and yet without judgment and strings. It was so different from the family I'd just left that it was almost laughable.

After opening the door, I pushed inside and leaned back against the cool wood, just breathing.

Why did I keep doing this to myself?

Why did I keep hoping things would be different, even while knowing they would always be the same?

My dad was my dad. He would always be ornery with a touch of mean. He'd never say *I love you* or *I'm proud of what you've done.* So, why did I keep looking for it? Why did I keep doing the same thing and hoping the outcome would be different? It was quite literally the definition of insanity.

And insane or not, I just didn't want to feel this way anymore.

I wanted my dad safe and healthy, but I didn't want my heart to feel like it had been put through the meat grinder every time we interacted.

It was the push-pull that was hard.

He always seemed to know exactly when I was ready to be done with him completely, to forget about Campbell and the ranch and him and just move on. And that was when I got some modicum of affection.

Reeling me back in.

Making me feel small.

I dropped my bag and sighed, knowing it wasn't just that, the crumbs of affection he doled out at irregular intervals. I was to blame, too. I was so starved for his love that I grasped at every straw.

But things were different now.

I had clients and friends. My life wasn't hollow any longer. Perhaps that was why the reminder of my empty relationship with my dad was so painful.

"Why can't I stop loving him?" I muttered, pushing off the door, scooping up my bag, and heading to the bedroom to repack it for the next time I'd need it. The dress I'd worn to the wedding was critically wrinkled and would need to be saved by the dry cleaner, but everything else was fine to either go into the hamper or the closet. I restocked my bag with clean underwear and socks, along with several staples that could be mixed and matched together to make an outfit appropriate for anything from a photo shoot to a nice dinner.

But even as my hands went through the motions of repacking my bag, my mind kept spinning.

I needed to find a way to break the pattern. I needed to stop feeling this way.

I needed . . . to come to terms with the fact that my father wasn't going to be the father I needed. But just thinking that, just having the thought cross my mind, sliced me to the quick. There was still hope inside me that things would change and—

I needed to let go of that.

I *had* to.

Sighing, I tugged the zipper closed, carried my bag to the little bench I kept by the front door—shoe storage below, a place to drop all the crap I needed to carry to my car at a later time on top.

This fell into the category of crap to bring to my car later.

Task done, I took a long, hot shower, washing off the travel, the weariness, the confusion that had morphed into resolve. I knew this was an exercise in futility, that I should shrug off the hope and move on, and I wanted it to be that simple. To just move on.

It wasn't.

But I'd also had enough.

So, even though the flame of hope in my gut wasn't quite extinguished, I was also done trying to add fuel to that fire, to encourage it to burn bigger and brighter. Time to accept and move on.

My cell buzzed, and I grabbed it, knowing that Talbot was supposed to be checking in soon after a series of interviews in Australia. He was on location for a couple more months of filming, even as another movie of his was releasing in theaters soon. It was my job to somehow balance his obligations of promotion and promote a reasonable work-life balance between that and starring in a film that was shooting an average of twelve-hour days.

The first step had been to set up some remote interviews with the bigger bloggers and promotion companies, allowing him to stay on set while honoring that part of his contract. Next, was to consolidate everything into a week of appearances on talk shows and only one junket, where he'd be available for a full day of short interviews with all the different entertainment shows and several large YouTubers.

This would make it so he only had to fly home once.

I glanced at the screen, saw instead of Talbot, it was a text from Tammy.

Delicious. Boys and I say thanks.

I smiled at the picture that accompanied the words, Tammy in her uniform, a slice of cinnamon apple bread in her hand, several crumb-filled pieces of foil on the table in the background. I typed a quick reply.

Sorry we couldn't grab a meal. Unfortunately, I had to get back.

No apologies necessary. There will be other times.

That I wasn't sure of.

Hope to see you in California soon.

A beat then:

Don't be a stranger. I miss having a friend I can talk ALL the shit with.

That made me grin and answer.

It's good we know our own strong points.

Word.

I was just typing up a response when my cell buzzed again.

Sorry to run. Duty calls.

Be safe. Talk soon.

Tammy didn't reply, and I set my phone on my nightstand, stomach rumbling, my emotions strung tight. I couldn't sit across the table from Artie and Pierce and perfect little Brenna and not feel lonely, not feel longing.

It wasn't that my biological clock was ticking—though I wasn't against the idea of having a kid any longer—rather, my friends were just such a solid unit. They knew each other in a deep, meaningful way, and that wasn't something I'd had, even with Aaron when we'd been together.

Maybe that wasn't fair.

Aaron and I *had* known each other deeply. It was just that our level of understanding, that deepness hadn't made any difference in the end, not when what we'd wanted was so mutually exclusive.

Stay. Go.

Family. Freedom.

Never would have worked.

I walked into the little kitchenette, fingers itching with the need to cook something, to bake anything, to focus on the ingredients, on the science, on things that made sense. If I added the right amount of baking soda, the loaves would rise. If I baked them too long, they would be dry. If I forgot to add eggs, they would be an utter disaster.

Flour, sugar, oil, and eggs into a homogenous mixture. Apples for moisture. Cinnamon for spice.

My cell rang as I was stirring everything together, Talbot calling in on FaceTime. I hit the button, grinned at his pajamas.

"You're wearing them," I exclaimed happily.

He wagged a finger at me, eyes narrowing. "You and I need to have a word, missy."

My stomach clenched, and I let the whisk fall into the bowl. "What's the problem?"

"The problem?" He threw up his hands, not helping my stomach-clenching issue. "The problem is that you bought me these stupidly expensive pajamas, and now my body revolts with anything less than the silky gloriousness on my skin."

I snorted, shook my head, lips curving despite the heaviness sitting on my heart. I loved this man so much.

He never failed to make me smile, never played the Hollywood ego, not that any of my clients did. I had too few hours in the day to deal with elitist bullshit, so I was choosy with who I took on.

"That's better," he said, face softening. "How are you, sweetheart?"

"I'm okay. I'm home."

"Did something—?"

"No." A shake of my head to accompany the lie, because a lot had fucking happened. "My dad's okay. It was just more comfortable for everyone if I came home early."

"Comfortable for him?" he asked. "Or for you?"

"How did the interviews go?" I replied rather than answering, going for subterfuge instead of truth.

He fixed me with a stare. "Maggie."

"What?"

"You're baking. You're home after a day, when you said you'd be gone a week. And I repeat," he said. "You're. Baking."

"I bake." Sometimes. Okay, hardly ever anymore. Only when I was really upset.

Which Talbot knew, since we'd share one too many old-fashioneds during our last press tour and had played two truths and a lie.

Ugh.

"Marjorie Allen—"

I scowled at the use of the full version of my old lady name. Marjorie made me feel like I should be wearing a house dress and curlers. "Remind me not to drink with you anymore."

"I like your name," he said. "It's classic and slides off the tongue like—"

"Interviews," I interrupted, not wanting to hear the rest of that sentence.

"*Baking*," he countered.

I sighed, knowing that while he might not have ego, he rivaled me in stubbornness. I either was going to give in and dish, or I'd need to hang up and silence my phone.

And if I took option two, I'd be fending off Artie in all of five minutes because he'd sic her on me if I tried to avoid him.

"You're the worst."

"*I'm* the client who made it through all the interviews without any snafus, who was charming and trustworthy, and who didn't insult a single person, either unintentionally or on purpose."

I tugged at my straight brown hair. "You want to make me go prematurely gray, don't you?"

He paused, considering. "I think you'd look cute gray." A beat. "Marjorie."

"Ugh!" I dropped the whisk into the bowl, picked up my cell, and stomped my way to the couch. "What? What do you want to know? That my dad was the same old mean bastard and I got my feelings hurt? That, worse, Aaron was there, and I—he—"

I dropped my chin to my chest.

"I'm sorry, babe," he murmured into the quiet. "You deserve better from your dad." He sighed. "But you know what my next question is going to be, right?"

I did.

I played dumb anyway. "So, things got tense and I came home. End of story. I'm going to work on not caring so much, on trying to accept that my dad and I won't have the type of relationship I crave."

Quiet. Then, "I'm glad, Mags. That's the right call, I think. But you also know that's not what I'm going to ask."

"I think I hear the timer," I said, standing. "I gotta go."

"Nice try, babe. You were still mixing when I called." His glare held me in place, even through the screen of my cell. "Who's Aaron?"

I wrinkled my nose, debated answering for a few more heartbeats then told him the truth. "My ex."

"I thought you didn't date."

"What?" I asked, shocked as I sank back down onto the couch cushions. "I date."

"Since when?" he countered. "I've never seen you with a man or woman who wasn't a client. And since Eden, Artie, and Pierce are married, and you're clearly not trying to get into *my* pants . . ."

He trailed off.

I frowned. "I have a life outside of you guys."

"Do you?" he asked. "Because while I know that Artie and Pierce have slowed their schedules in the last few years, Eden and I are busy as ever."

"I date," I replied stubbornly.

"Are you counting attending a work function and talking to another man, or woman, as a date?"

I was. Dammit.

"That's not the point."

Talbot snorted. "That's *exactly* the point."

"Snorting isn't cute," I said.

"Good thing I don't care about being cute, and even if I did, I have a talented publicist to help me figure that out," he said and added, voice gentling, "One who any man or woman would be lucky to date."

"Man," I said. One in particular, who made my heart alternate between aching and skipping a beat, who sent my nerves into shock, who filled me with longing. And memories. And wishes that somehow things could have been different.

"What?"

"I'm attracted to men. Just for the record. I like men."

"Ah, so ex-Aaron is Aaron with an A."

"Yeah." I pushed to my feet again, crossed to the kitchen, well aware my tone sounded miserable.

"That good, huh?"

"I'll remind you that I bake to forget my f-feelings," I told him, hating when I faltered over the last word, misery trailing through me again. "Not to relive them."

"Babe."

I sighed. "Aaron and I were high school sweethearts, okay? He wanted to get married. I wanted to live a bigger life. He's still living in Utah and is the one who called to tell me my dad was in the hospital," I said, giving Talbot the Cliffs Notes version. Then I shook my head and positioned the phone near my mixing bowl. "He's also never forgiven me for breaking things off between us, and he had some choice words to say when I saw him at the house."

"Asshole."

I shook my head. "Unfortunately, not. He's hurt. I broke *his* dream to take *mine*."

"That's bullshit."

"Not bullshit," I said. "But also not fair of him," I added when Tal would have continued protesting. "Still, I said my piece, told him he needed to get over it, and move on like an adult." I shrugged. "Not sure any of that got through, but I'm at as much peace about it as I can be. I didn't want to hurt him, and I'm sorry he *was* hurt. But even if I could go back and change the past, I wouldn't." I smiled at my friend through the phone. "I like my life now."

"Mags."

Please don't push for more details.

I didn't think I had the strength to churn them all up again, not when they'd been a constant rejoinder for the last day and a half.

"I love you."

My breath caught. There was a reason he was the biggest star right now. Tal was gorgeous, sweet, and could be all too charming. "Too bad you're not single," I said, picking up the whisk and starting to stir.

He grinned, but it was a brief flash before concern bled through his expression. "You sure you're good?"

I nodded. "I'm fine."

Or I *would* be fine. Eventually.

Talbot was quiet for a few more moments and when I heard him start to speak again, I braced myself. As mentioned, he rivaled me in stubbornness, and I really just wanted to forget my old life back in Utah for a bit. Not avoidance so much as self-preservation.

Thankfully when he began talking again, it was about work.

He filled me in on the interviews, highlighting the key points, telling me that my new assistant, Sam, who was cutting his teeth on his first big solo PR gig, had done a pretty good job of keeping everyone on topic and on time. I was thrilled to hear it. Sam had sent a report to me via email, but nothing really mattered unless the client was happy.

"I'm glad," I said when he paused for air.

"Me, too."

I opened my mouth, ready to tell him I was going to let him go, but then Talbot transitioned from business into a hilarious anecdote about the director, who was apparently scared of flies, lurching off his chair in the middle of a shot, dumping it over and frightening the cast and crew half to death before running in circles to, "Get it away. Get it away!"

By the time the reenactment was done, I was in stitches, tears pouring down my cheeks.

"I shouldn't laugh," I said. "But . . ."

Talbot was chuckling, too. "I know, but I feel okay doing it now. Especially since we took care of the fly, and Ralph spent the rest of the day poking fun at his phobia."

"That's good."

He nodded, and I smiled at him, the ache in my heart not quite as painful.

"I know what you're doing," I told him, wishing he was here so I could give him a hug.

"Yeah, what's that?" he asked, all innocent.

I shook my head. "Thanks, Tal."

His expression gentled. "Anytime, babe." Then he grinned, mischief back on his face. "Just so you're aware, I ordered a giant blow-up fly to be delivered to set tomorrow."

I burst out laughing. "They have those?"

"They sure do. In fact, they have all sorts of blow-up animals . . ."

I listened to him talk as I poured the batter into the loaf pans, as I slid them into the oven, as I set the timer and waited.

And by the time we hung up, my baked loaves were cooling on the counter, and I didn't feel flayed open any longer.

I was stitched back together.

My family, my real family, had done that.

SEVEN

Aaron

"SHE'S TRASH, I TELL YOU," Warren muttered, hobbling in through the door to the bunkhouse.

"Claudette?" I asked, familiar enough with the Warren Show at the moment to know he was unhappy having a nurse ordering him around.

"No," Warren snapped, eyes darting around the room, as though he was uncertain for a moment where he was, but before that inkling really processed, his next words had me reeling. "The other one . . . my daughter."

Was this a She-Who-Shall-Not-Be-Named situation?

But I had work to do, and so I needed to kindly kick Warren out of here. Once, this had been the perfect partnership, the two of us in league railing against the unjust world . . . or really, the unfairness that was Mags leaving. Now, that was getting a little old.

Especially as several weeks had gone by, and I couldn't get her words out of my head. Was I to blame? The logical part of my mind told me it made sense—

Shaking myself, I tuned back to Warren, just in time to hear, "And did you know, she told Claudette to make sure I'm taking my medication?" He huffed. "Like I'm a child. She's the child. She's the piece of trash I should have gotten rid of long ago."

Fury.

Not at Maggie, but at Warren.

She might not be in Utah every weekend, but she did a good job of taking care of the old man, especially when he didn't *want* to be taken care of, when he fought her about everything from the gardener to the housecleaner to the guy who'd come out to clean the gutters.

"I should have thrown—"

"Don't," I gritted out.

Warren's gaze found his. "What?"

"Don't say that about Maggie."

He sniffed. "I can say what I want."

"Not around me." Not any longer. Not when her words were running through my mind every night when I went to bed. Not when, with each day that passed, it was harder and harder to deny she was right.

"I can do what I want," Warren muttered, but he turned away, headed for the door before I had a chance to rebut that. "Stupid hands. Always overstepping. Never know their boundary."

I frowned as the door slammed behind him, thinking it had been a long time since I'd been simply a hand helping out on this ranch.

But also . . . Warren was Warren.

Crochety. Inexplicable. *Warren.*

Sighing, I opened my laptop, took a few moments to find my place again, and got back to work.

It had been three weeks since I'd come back to the ranch and found Warren splayed on the concrete, and I was getting the hell out of Dodge.

Storms were coming in regular intervals, snow was piled high on the side of every road, and Warren was back on his feet, slightly wobbling but doing a good enough job of getting himself around the house.

Though, I couldn't say I'd had much to do with that.

Claudette had driven him home from the hospital and promptly taken over, running the ranch with an iron fist I'd come to respect. I'd spent my days in meetings and going over reports, but now, my business in town was completed, and I was ready for my next round of travel.

Even after nearly eight years in the business, I still wasn't quite sure how I'd fallen into the wine industry. Of course, I *knew* how, but it was still almost a surprise when I thought about what I did for a living.

But here I was with vineyards in Italy, France, Utah, and . . . California.

Temecula. Southern California's wine country and the location where our biggest seller was grown.

Our Chardonnay had a velvety texture and just the right amount of sweetness.

But, surprisingly, our Utah varieties were taking off. I'd thought it a bizarre crop for the state when I'd first snagged a summer job at the only winery nearby between my freshman and sophomore years of college. The man who'd owned it, Carlos, was eccentric, to say the least, and everyone in town thought he was insane for picking Utah, even crazier for growing something called ice wine.

The grapes were harvested in December or January, when they froze on the vine, and then pressed for juice still frozen. It made for an intensely sweet wine, albeit unusual. But as the market had grown for the variety, Carlos had taken me under his wing. I was a business major with my eye on an MBA; he was the green thumb. We'd become partners—hello, student loans—but it had funded both my education and was an investment into the business.

And then the business had paid off my loans.

And then we'd bought into Temecula.

Then France in the Loire Valley. Finally, Italy in Abruzzo.

Carlos had returned to his native Italy to manage our European investments, and I'd stayed on to manage the U.S. side. We still crossed paths regularly, both making sure to keep our fingers on the pulse of all our locations, but the division of locations suited us . . . and the variation in time zones.

My business partner was still eccentric and experimental, but we'd both worked like hell to build our own slice of the wine industry, our tiny empire of four wineries. Kings of the Grapes, as Carlos liked to say.

I figured I was more the King of the Spreadsheets, but I let Carlos do his thing.

For now, our Utah grapes were nearly ready for harvest, and the staff here had things well in hand. So, I was heading out to California to meet with my marketing team and an actor they wanted to utilize to help promote our wines. After that, I would walk through and approve, hopefully, a new planting area we were going to seed in the spring. Fires had taken out a chunk of our vines the previous year, and if we were investing in rebuilding part of the acreage, Carlos and I wanted to make sure the money was worth it.

Okay, *I* wanted to make sure the money was worth it.

Carlos had walked the grounds in bare feet and declared, "This is the spot."

Luckily for me, and the reason our business had been successful so far, was that Carlos *could* be reasoned with if logistics proved impossible. However, that was rarely necessary, because Carlos's bare feet technique was damned near infallible.

I zipped up my suitcase and straightened, hoping it would be infallible in this case, too.

I was exhausted.

But then again, not sleeping would do that to a man.

I wanted to blame it on worry for Warren or perhaps me finally having the urge to invest in a house or build a space at the winery where I could stay during the few months I was in town.

That blame would be misplaced.

I'd been thinking of Maggie. Constantly.

Hearing her words, her certainty, and at first being so fucking pissed that she'd dared put any responsibility of ending us on me. Then staring at that circle of metal, the tiny peach with its equally tiny diamond, and realizing she'd kept it all these years.

And slowly, infinitesimally coming to the conclusion that she was right.

We'd been at two dramatically different places in life, and, frankly, it was unfair for me to have put pressure on her to stay just because *I* wanted her to.

I could have gone.

We could have tried to make things work long-distance.

But I would have eventually become resentful. At that point, I *hadn't* wanted to leave or see the world or be with anyone else. I'd wanted to go to college in Salt Lake. I'd wanted to get my degree, find a job in town or nearby, and buy a house with a picket fence on the same street as my parents. I hadn't had big dreams. And, maybe this sounded awful, because I did love her, but part of it had also been that Mags was comfortable and easy and *mine*. It had made sense for us to take the next step. Was totally logical.

Made. Sense. Logical.

All the things a young woman with her mind on the future, who'd had the big dreams I hadn't, wouldn't want to hear.

So, yeah, I'd come to the conclusion that I was a fucking idiot at eighteen, thinking I knew all the right things to do, that I knew best.

It wasn't until my mom got sick about nine months after Maggie was gone that I'd started to mature. And it wasn't until I'd devoted countless hours to a job and business that I'd begun to possess a modicum of adulthood, to understand that just because I had wanted something didn't mean the world owed it to me.

And now I realized that even though we'd spent four years together as boyfriend and girlfriend, even though we'd been each other's firsts in so many ways—first love, first kiss, first time—Maggie didn't owe me anything.

She hadn't snuck off. She hadn't made promises and left in the middle of the night.

She'd told me for *years* that her plan was to move to California after she turned eighteen, and I'd watched her for *years* as she'd saved money from every babysitting job, every birthday and holiday, every shift at Henry's Diner she'd worked in the next town over to make that happen.

And somehow, I'd still been surprised that she'd gone.

Look, it didn't feel great to know that I wasn't enough to make her want to stay, and I knew now that part of the reason I'd held on to the anger was because of ego. Or rather, *my* ego being bruised.

But . . . that conversation in the kitchen, seeing her spine go ramrod stiff like she was afraid I was going to cut her down and it was the only way for her to stay strong. Seeing her pull into herself because I'd acted like her dad—

Fuck. I didn't want to turn into Warren.

I'd respected him at one point. He'd let me stay at the ranch, had given me some comfort—even if it was comfort in anger—after Mags had gone.

But I didn't want to be a gruff, ornery bastard who didn't have anything except some property and an empty house. I wanted a full life, with a family that was my own. I was too old to be carrying a bruised heart from a decade before. Mags' words might not have taken in that moment, but the last three weeks with nothing but my spreadsheets and the quiet of the ranch, and I'd started to see things through a different lens.

Either you would have had to sacrifice what you wanted, or I would have had to.

What did a pair of eighteen-year-olds know about sacrifice? Well, *she'd* clearly known more than me, with my happily married parents, with my stable family, my siblings who all got along. I'd known I was loved from the first moment I could remember. Mags had always struggled to see through Warren's gruff.

A gruff that was getting sharper as the years progressed.

It was something I'd tried to tell the old man as the years had gone on, but Mags had gotten her stubborn from somewhere, and that somewhere was Warren.

He was of the tough, I-don't-express-my-feelings set, and Maggie, who'd lost her mom, who was an only child in a new town, had needed more feelings. I knew that was part of why she'd left, that searching and aching and craving something more fulfilling from her dad.

And just not finding it.

"Yet, you held her leaving against her for a solid decade, dumbass," I muttered, grabbing my suitcase by the handle and running through my mental to-do list, trying to stop going around and around in my mind for the umpteenth time in the last few weeks.

The past was the past.

She'd made the right choice in going. I was man enough to accept that now.

I made my way over to the coffee pot, exorcised from the house by nurse Claudette since coffee didn't fit in with Warren's post-heart attack diet. Something he'd known, apparently, but had just bided his time after the last time the nurse had been at the house, waiting until she'd finished her tenure before buying a new maker and resuming his morning cup of joe. I still felt a little guilty for having spent so much time with Warren and not having known that, but part of me recognized that even if I *had* known, I still probably wouldn't have fought the old bugger over one cup a day.

My lips ghosted up as I filled my mug.

Claudette had no compunction over fighting with Warren though.

And Warren had no compunction over giving in. In fact, he even seemed to relish in Claudette taking care of him.

Which made no logical sense. Mags had been here to do the same thing, and she perhaps had more of a claim to provide that care, considering she was his daughter, but I'd given up a while ago on understanding what made Warren tick. Of course, I should have given up *before* I'd broached the subject of what had happened with Maggie at the hospital the night of his surgery.

Unfortunately for me and my eardrums, I hadn't.

"Lesson learned," I muttered before taking a gulp of coffee. I was allowed to hang around as long as I didn't *pester him.*

His words.

That had been trailed by *otherwise, you can get your own damned place and get the hell off my ranch.*

Ah. Warren.

To which I had countered with, *don't worry, the next time I'm in town, I'll stay at the winery.*

Warren had glared. I had retreated to my laptop.

Because . . . had I really related to that fury inside the older man for nearly a decade?

It shamed me to think that I had, almost as much as it shamed me that I hadn't understood exactly why Mags had left Campbell until that morning in Warren's kitchen three weeks before.

But what could I do at this point?

She was gone. I didn't have access to her number without hijacking Warren's cell, or address, at least not without asking Warren for it, and neither of those was a road I was willing to travel down.

The past.

All in the past. If I saw Mags again, I'd apologize. Let her know that I was sorry it had taken me so long to get my head out of my ass, but that I got it and I wish I'd done things differently.

Let her know that the person I'd been mad at all these years wasn't her.

I'd finally realized it was me.

My cell buzzed as I was rinsing my glass and cleaning up the rest of the space, making sure no critters would be attracted to any crumbs when I left. Eyeing the space for any left-behind belongings, I tugged the phone from my pocket, swiped without looking at the screen, and brought it up to my ear, I barely got my "Hello?" out before my mom's voice came through the speaker.

"I thought you were coming by for breakfast."

I grinned, shook my head. She always made me feel about ten, and even though I was nearly thirty and somehow reduced to a tween by just her voice, I loved the woman to the moon and back.

"Pushy," I teased.

"You love me," she teased back. "Pancakes are going on the griddle in five. It's on you if they're cold and soggy by the time you get here."

"I'm just cleaning up the bunkhouse," I told her, drying and putting the mug and coffee pot away, taking the dirty linens from the bed and bagging them. I'd drop them by the dry cleaner on the way to the airport, where they'd launder and hold on to them until I came back to Campbell. "I'm out the door in five."

"Make it four."

I laughed. "I know you still operate on military time, Mom, but I'll be there as soon as I can."

"Five kids, I *had* to operate on military time."

"I love you," I said, grabbing a sock I'd somehow missed and shoving it into my suitcase. "Your military time is distracting me. I'll see you in a few."

"Love you, baby boy. See you in a bit." A beat. "But the pancakes may still be cold."

I laughed as I said my goodbye and hung up, knowing that the pancakes wouldn't be cold, that they'd be steaming and fluffy and delicious, not only because my mom was a great cook, but because she wouldn't put the batter on the griddle until she heard my car pull into the driveway, timing it so the hot circles of yumminess hit my plate at the perfect moment.

My mom was incredible.

But my mom was also part of why I hadn't understood what Maggie had been going through until she'd spelled it out for me like the dumbass I was in the kitchen three weeks ago.

I'd had perfectly-timed pancakes. She'd had . . . Warren.

Sighing, knowing there wasn't anything I could do about that or the fact that this wasn't new information, I pocketed my cell and used one hand to pick up the bagged linens, used my other to heft my suitcase, and made my way to the door.

Lights off.

Door locked, more because I found myself thinking the habit Mags had picked up in L.A. was a smart one rather than because there was any great risk that someone would enter the space uninvited.

Even when I wasn't directly thinking about her, she was in my brain. What a mess.

Sighing, I headed out to my car.

My mom was driving me to the airport after breakfast and would take my car back to their house and store it until I came back to town. My dad would start it at regular intervals, would hook up a backup battery charger so it didn't run dead while not in use.

Family.

Mine was great.

Mags' was—

"Fuck," I gritted out, tossing the suitcase and bag of linens into the trunk and slamming it shut. I got in my driver's seat, Warren and I having said our goodbyes the night before over Claudette's surprisingly tasty low-fat casserole, and I didn't bother to glance at, let alone go up to the main house.

He wouldn't want another conversation.

"Waste of time saying goodbye twice," I could imagine him growling.

Which was just as well. I had pancakes to get to.

As PREDICTED, the pancakes were piping hot and perfectly fluffy, making their way onto my plate just as I strolled through the door.

"Hi, honey," my mom said, walking over to the bar-top counter of the island and setting the plate alongside a napkin already prepped with a knife and fork. I inhaled the delicious scent of pancakes, of bacon and eggs, and knew I was a nearly thirty-year-old man who'd been spoiled for most of my life.

Not that I was complaining.

The difference is that even as my mom, my parents, my siblings spoiled me, I spoiled them right back.

Case in point, the barstool I was plunking my ass into.

I'd paid for it. Well, I'd paid for everything in the kitchen. The stools, the countertops, the appliances, the cabinets. I'd hired a contractor to create my mom's dream kitchen three years ago.

Five years in remission deserved a celebration.

And since she wouldn't let me buy her a vacation to the Caribbean or Europe, like she'd always wanted to go, I'd gotten her appliances.

Oh, she'd still protested *that*.

But then I'd bought the stove I knew she'd always wanted—a huge unit with two ovens, six burners, a grill, and a separate griddle—and had it delivered to the house for Christmas.

It had barely fit through the door.

But she'd fallen in love, had practically salivated over using it.

So when I'd threatened her with the matching fridge, dishwasher, and microwave, she'd relented and let the contractor come and plan the space.

I think it was the double oven that pushed her over the edge.

Either way, I knew, digging into my pancakes, I was really the one who benefited.

Home-cooked meals.

A happy mom.

Yeah, it had been well worth the money.

She filled her own plate and came to sit next to me. "What time's your flight?"

"Eleven." I took a bite. "Thanks for driving me."

"Of course, baby." Her fingers brushed across my forehead, a light touch she'd done for as long as I could remember. It was something I'd once shied away from, a babyish bit of contact to retreat from or block, thinking I was too old for it.

Then I'd almost lost it.

So, now I knew how precious that touch was.

And after the quiet contemplation of the last weeks, now I wondered if Mags had ever had it.

I'd touched her, of course. But the caress of a boyfriend who wanted to get into her pants was markedly different than that of a parent, of a mom.

She'd never had the latter, and I couldn't see Warren kissing booboos.

Fuck.

It had been easier when I'd been wrapped up in myself. Thinking like this, recognizing all the things I'd missed as a teenager more wrapped up in myself than the world around me, and I was feeling no little amount of guilt.

I should have been better.

Or at the very least, it shouldn't have taken me ten years to realize that my pain, my hurt wasn't bigger than Maggie's.

Sometimes things didn't work out, but that didn't mean one of us had to be a monster or a bad guy—

"You've got some really heavy thoughts running through your mind."

I glanced up from my pancakes, saw my mom had set down her fork. "I'm okay, Mom. Thanks for breakfast. It's delicious, as always."

"I'm glad you say you're okay." She picked up her fork. "But my Mom Powers tell me otherwise. And you know that I won't push you to talk," she added when I opened my mouth to demure.

No. She wouldn't.

My mom wasn't the *overtly* pushy type. More the sly pushy. Not demanding I tell her what was wrong. Instead, she would remind me she was there to listen, and she would make herself available so that by the time the feelings needed an out, she was always nearby. So really, she just out-patienced me into confessing what was wrong. Or maybe out-pancaked me, I realized, since the revelations usually came over breakfast.

"How do you always know?" I asked, setting down my own fork.

Her lips quirked. "Are you questioning my Mom Powers?"

"The ones that always knew when I was even a minute past curfew?" I asked teasingly. "No. I wouldn't be stupid enough to do that."

"Smart boy."

I grabbed our plates, now empty, and carried them to the sink then returned for the utensils and coffee mugs. "Want a refill?" I asked.

"No, honey."

Since I'd had enough caffeine to feel a bit jittery, I dumped the contents from both mugs in the sink and began washing up. Or maybe it was less the caffeine and more related to the fact that I was about to say, just loud enough to be heard over the running water, "I saw Maggie."

Silence.

I washed the first dish, stuck it in the dishwasher. Then repeated the pattern with the second, with the pan from the eggs and bacon, though those I dried with a hand towel and put away. When I turned back to face my mom at the bar top, she was studying me carefully.

"And how'd that make you feel?"

"Pissed."

Her eyes clouded.

"At first."

They cleared.

"We said some things. Well, no, I barked at her and she returned some calm volleys that made me think."

"Think?" my mom asked. "Or reconsider?"

"Think," I said. "Think myself into circles before I realized that I needed to reconsider everything I'd felt and thought after she left."

"Why?"

I frowned. "Why?"

"You guys exchanged plenty of words *before* she left."

I chuckled darkly, remembering those words had been more argument than thoughtful exchange.

She patted my hand when I came to lean against the counter near her. "Why did these words affect you?"

I sighed. "Probably because I've realized she was right." I slipped my hand into my pocket, to where I'd stashed the charm bracelet, rolling the peach between my thumb and forefinger, and knowing that this, too, had played a part in my revised thinking. She'd kept it all these years because it was important. She hadn't thrown it away. She hadn't thrown *me* away.

"Oh, baby," my mom murmured and squeezed my fingers again. "You were both young. Mistakes were made on both sides."

I made a face. "I know that."

"But you think that you made bigger ones?" she asked, proving her Mom Powers were real by poaching the thoughts right from my mind.

"How can I not?" I asked. "It wasn't like Mags ever hid what she wanted."

"A big city. A big career in Hollywood."

I nodded. "I held that against her, tried to make her dreams smaller so they'd fit with mine. I loved her, but just as much as I cared for her, I think I was almost more hurt that I wasn't big enough to fill her hopes for the future and resentful that she wanted something else." A sigh. "I should have recognized that really loving someone meant not trying to shrink them down, to make their dream more palatable. It's accepting them, helping to make them happen."

My mom was quiet for a long time, then she slipped her hand free from mine. "And did you tell her that when you talked?" she asked.

"I told her . . ." I sighed, admitted, "Pretty much as far from that as possible."

She smiled. "Ah. My baby boy, Aaron, stubborn from the time you came to life in my womb. Don't make that face," she said when I'd apparently let my uneasiness at the word *womb* coming from my mom's mouth—*shudder*—bleed through my expression. "You're like your father in many ways. Smart, passionate, hard-working, but you're also like me."

"Wonderful? Loving? Makes awesome pancakes?"

A tap on her nose. "Got two out of three, baby," she said, lips tipped up at the edges. "The third way you're like me is your mad stubborn skills."

I snorted. "Rose"—my younger sister—"is a bad influence on you."

"She's keeping me young." A flash of a smile. "But stubborn isn't always a bad thing, no matter how much your dad likes to tease me. It's what got me through cancer. It's what helped you build your business. But, it's also something we can hold on to blindly, something that can hurt more than push forward."

"I'm not sure I'd call you fighting cancer as stubborn." I slipped my arm around her shoulders. "I think it's because you're strong as hell."

"I'll take that," she said, "but it doesn't preclude my point."

"Yeah," I muttered. "Unfortunately, my stubborn meant that it took me three weeks from the conversation to realize that Mags had several valid points, and the biggest of those being that I'd been eighteen and stupid and we wouldn't have worked out anyway."

"I'm not sure I believe that. Things could have—"

I glanced at the clock, interrupted, albeit gently. "We should go."

She kept her eyes on me for a heartbeat then nodded, slipping from the stool and starting to gather up her purse and jacket. I trailed her to the door, opening and closing it for her, then repeating the action when we'd made it to my car.

"How long until you're back?" she asked once we were driving down the street, heading for a quick pit stop at the dry cleaners.

"I might be here for a weekend if the harvest comes in at the right time between L.A. and France. Otherwise, I'll be in for Christmas."

"Good."

Quiet fell, not uncomfortable, but my mom was deep in thought. Fine by me, as mine was dominated by a particular brunette who'd only grown more beautiful over the last ten years. I parked at the curb by the dry cleaners, ran the bag of linens inside.

"Did you know that Maggie came to visit me in the hospital after my surgery?" she asked as I buckled back in and pulled back onto the road.

My heart skipped a beat, and I nearly swerved out of my lane.

"Um. *No,*" I said, forcing my tone to be calm. "I— that's— it doesn't . . ." I trailed off because it was what? Shocking? Painful? Unsurprising? "Why didn't you tell me?" I eventually asked.

"She asked me not to," my mom said softly. "She'd pawned her car to pay for the plane ticket back."

Forget skipping a beat. Now my heart seized. "She sold her car?"

A nod. "Wouldn't let me give her money for a new one or at least a down payment for something that wasn't a clunker." My mom rotated in her seat, gaze meeting mine for a split second before my eyes returned to the road. "I told her to go and not come back."

Now it took every bit of my concentration to stay straight in my lane. *"What?"*

Her hand came to my arm, gripping lightly. "Maggie needed to look forward instead of worrying about everything behind her." Her fingers slid away. "It was the right call for both of you. I still think that, and perhaps that's *my* stubborn talking. Maybe I overstepped, but Aaron, I worried for both of you. Worried what might happen if you two continued to tangle each other up and get pulled back into the past." She sighed. "I'd hoped that once she fulfilled those big dreams, she would come back."

"But she didn't."

"No." Eyes on her hands, voice quiet. "But do you know that she's sent me a postcard from every place she's visited?" A beat. "It's a *lot* of places."

I took the exit for the airport, mind spinning as her next words came.

"Just like you, honey. You've lived some big dreams, ones you never even knew you wanted," she said, still soft. "Only now, I think you understand the value of those big dreams. You've traveled and lived . . . and you'll both be in the same place." Her hand found mine again. "Now, you can do something about this new knowledge. Now, you can put some of your stubborn to good use."

"Southern California is a big place."

She sighed. "It's not *that* big. Don't try and find an excuse to keep avoiding your life."

I checked for traffic behind me and changed lanes, not arguing with the last statement. It was true, that much had been blatantly spelled out to me three weeks before, had been pounded home into my brain with my constant thinking.

"Even if she would let me see her and apologize, I don't know if she's in town. And I have no clue where she lives," I said, navigating us to the terminal. "I don't even have her number." I pulled to stop, turned to face my mom, who'd pulled out her cell, fingers moving on the screen. "Somehow I doubt it's listed."

My own phone buzzed.

My mom's mouth turned up. "Funny story . . ." she said, unbuckling her seat belt as I did the same then shifted to retrieve my cell from my pocket. My brows drew together when I saw the text was from her. "I have Maggie's number." She pressed a kiss to my cheek. "And now you do, too."

Breath catching, I wasn't able to form a response as she leaned back and opened the passenger's side door. My eyes were locked on the screen, on the name in the contact my mom had just shared with me.

Maggie Allen.

Pulse skipping, heat trailing down my spine.

The sound of the car's trunk opening finally tore my eyes from the screen. I hurried out my door, moving to grab my suitcase before my mom tried to and hurt herself.

She smiled when I nudged her out of the way.

"You're a good man, Aaron."

I'd thought so, but the last few weeks had made me wonder. Now, hearing the surety in her tone relaxed some knot inside me I hadn't even realized I'd been holding on to.

She closed the trunk once I'd retrieved my bag, waited until

I'd made it to the curb before tugging me down for a hug. "I love you," she murmured into my ear.

"I love you, too."

She released me, stepped back. "Now, go forth and use *your* powers for good."

I snorted.

"That means *text* her." A pause, eyes sparkling with mischief. "Or better yet, forget all this newfangled texting and just *call* her."

I shook my head, smiling despite myself. "Bye, Mom."

A pat to my arm as she headed for the driver's door. "Bye, baby."

"Mom?" I called as she started to get in.

"Yeah?"

I held up my cell. "Thanks."

She grinned. "Anytime, honey."

I watched her drive away then headed into the terminal for my flight. But while my body was firmly in security then waiting at the gate, my mind was on a whole other plane of existence, no pun intended. Because . . . I was with Maggie. With her words and the past. With those words and the possibility of where they might lead us in the future.

I needed all my *powers* to craft the perfect text.

EIGHT

Maggie

What would you say if I told you that you were right and I was wrong?

I ROLLED OVER IN BED, eyes bleary from the late event the night before, and squinted at the text on my screen. The number wasn't in my contacts, and I cautiously opened the message for fear of random dick pics.

Thankfully, it was just that single question.

"Weird," I muttered, shoving out of bed and thinking about the date I'd gone on the previous evening.

Not quite a disaster, but close.

Troy was gorgeous, smart, and had held down a solid job for several years, but he'd also spent the entirety of the appetizers and main course talking about himself.

I got nerves. I understood that sometimes they made people babble.

This was *beyond* babbling.

Although, I now knew everything I thought I could comprehend about writing code to select the largest number in an array, something he'd apparently used to test a prospective employee in an interview that afternoon.

Though, I should probably admit, all I'd been able to process was that an array involved a grouping of numbers.

Look, I got numbers, but they were usually in social media followers, in views on a video, in a high Q Score—a quotient of likeability brands and celebrities used to measure their appeal and familiarity. But I got lost in the math of calculating that Q Score and most definitely in writing an equation to select for the largest number in a series of numbers.

Why I couldn't just look at them and point out the biggest one was beyond me.

But then again, I wasn't the mathematician.

Anyway, eventually I'd gotten tired of hearing about it and had made my excuses, planning on sitting in the hot tub and drinking a bottle of wine.

Pierce, Artie, and Brenna were traveling, and I had been alone, and well . . . one bottle had turned into two. Which meant I'd stayed up too late and drank too much and—hello, too bright morning and hangover central.

So, the knock at the door was not welcome.

"Ugh," I groaned, pulling the pillow over my head.

Unfortunately, it didn't drown out the sound of the knocking.

"Son of a goddamned array," I muttered, shoving the covers back, "And two fucking bottles of chardonnay—" I paused, shook my head at the bad rhyme and pushed myself out of bed. One quick glance to determine that I was decent enough to answer the door, another to look at the clock.

Seven-thirty.

Seven-freaking-thirty in the morning when I'd been up until

. . . two? No, three. I distinctly remembered looking at the time before I went to bed.

The knocking increased in volume and my annoyance flared. "I'm coming!" I called.

Okay, yelled.

Either way, it had the desired effect of cutting off the incessant noise as I made my way down the short hall that led to the front door of the guest house.

The security guards traveled with Pierce and Artie, but the system was still active and monitored when they weren't home. Since I hadn't gotten a call from the security company or an alert in the guest house's separate system, I could safely assume I knew the knocker and that they were most likely on the approved visitor's list.

I still peeked through the window to make sure most likely was actually true.

It was.

"Talbot!" I gasped, flinging the door open. "Didn't you just get in late last night? Is everything okay?"

"Fine, babe." He slipped past me, leaving me standing in the open door.

I rolled my eyes, knowing from that single sentence that nothing was *fine,* and shut the door behind me. "What's wrong?"

"Nothing," he said again. Except his gaze was deliberately pointing away from me, circling the room like he'd never been in the space, when in actuality he'd crashed on my couch not that long ago, when a pipe had burst in his brand-new house in West Hollywood.

"Tal."

"I'm fine."

"Tal."

He finally turned his head so I could see his face. His expression wasn't pretty.

"You didn't come here this early in the morning because everything is fine," I said. "What's happened?"

A sigh. Then, "Kasey happened."

Kasey was his girlfriend, and I was not a fan, to say the least.

"What do you mean?" I asked carefully, trying not to make a face, even as I struggled to keep my voice neutral.

"Shooting wrapped early, and I took an earlier flight to surprise her—"

"Oh, no," I said, a sinking feeling in my stomach telling me where this was going.

He turned away, thrust a hand through his hair. "This shit is only supposed to happen in movies."

"Was it that bad?"

"If you mean bad in the sense that I walked through the front door and found her fucking my assistant in the middle of my newly completed staircase," he gritted out. "Then yes, it was that bad."

"Didn't you tell me it was all wood and steel?" I asked then shook myself because that was *so* not the point.

Anger had hardened the lines of his handsome face, but my asinine and unnecessary question softened them with confusion. "What?"

"No, sorry," I said. "That was . . . uncalled for."

His head tilted to the side. "No, Mags. Tell me."

I wrinkled my nose. "It's just . . . that doesn't seem comfortable. To be"—I waved a hand up and down, cheeks flaring hot, not able to believe I'd gone there with a client—"having relations on something that's hard and made of wood and steel."

Talbot froze.

"See?" I pointed out. "Uncalled for."

His lips twitched. "Relations?"

My cheeks went hot. "You may be my friend, but you're my client first. I was trying to be professional."

He snorted. "That's not you."

Ouch. Averting my gaze, I started to shift backward, already thinking up the guise of needing to grab my cell from the bedroom, knowing that I could take thirty seconds and pull myself together because I'd done it time and again in my life.

First, get away from the person who hurt me.

Second, find a quiet and separate space.

Third, breathe and hold back any unplanned and unnecessary tears.

I'd gotten really good at those three steps over the years.

Today, the steps proved unnecessary.

"And it's not me," Talbot went on before I could carry them out. "For one, you saw me puking my guts up because I ate too many crab legs at the free buffet at my first real Hollywood party. For another, you covered me when my tuxedo slacks ripped, and I almost flashed the red carpet. Not to mention the time you snuck me out the back of the club downtown when I had a few too many tequila shots and got sloppy." His brows dragged down. "Come to think of it, maybe you *are* the professional one. You always seem to be rescuing me."

I shrugged, relief filling me. "That's my job."

It shouldn't really matter what this man thought of me, but Talbot was my boss, my friend, my family, and if he thought of me like my dad did—a flighty, useless nuisance, then I was mature enough to admit it would hurt.

A lot.

"Not your job, sweetheart," he said. "I know I'm lucky to have you. We're family, more than either of us have." He chucked me under the chin, his expression soft and not hiding the pain in his eyes. His childhood and mine were very similar, and probably also one of the reasons we'd clicked from the get-go. "So anyway, things between us aren't always professional, and I'm glad for it." He slung an arm over my shoulders, making my breath hitch, making those tears that I was so good at holding back dry in an instant.

"We are good at polishing off bottles of alcohol," I said.

He laughed but broke off with a groan.

"What's the matter?" I asked, turning to face him, cupping his cheeks, feeling his forehead. "Are you sick?"

"Not sick." He dropped his chin to his chest. "I forgot Ben"—his manager—"set up a business meeting at a winery today. I'm supposed to talk with their owners, see if I'm the right fit for the face of their brand."

That was strange.

One, that no one had run it by me. Two, for a wine company to want to pay a celebrity to market their wine was unusual. I would have expected a tequila or even a whiskey. A wine was . . . okay, I guessed. I would have preferred some time to process the brand implications.

"When was the meeting set?" I asked, starting with the most pressing issue. If someone on Talbot's team was trying to circumvent me, I had a bigger problem than fitting wine in with a brand.

"Maybe three weeks ago. Sam handled the details—" He broke off. "Shoot. You didn't know?"

I shook my head. "I'm guessing it all came together when I was in Utah."

"Yeah. That's when it was relayed to me." He squeezed my shoulders. "Sorry you were blindsided."

"It's fine." I waved a hand. "Okay, so based on what you walked into, I'm guessing you want to cancel the meeting."

"Yes," he said. "I mean, no, I won't cancel, of course. It's just . . . Kasey was supposed to go with me. It's some sort of couple's tasting we're trying out."

"I'll go with you."

"No—"

I stepped out from under his arm, rotated to fix him with a glare. "What time is the meeting?"

A hesitation.

I gave him Mean Publicist eyes, and he caved, just like I'd know he would. "Ten-thirty."

"Where?"

"Temecula."

I shifted so I could see the clock above the oven. It was already eight, and by the time I showered off any lingering traces of hangover and pulled myself into some semblance of order—which meant less pajamas and more professional clothes and makeup—it would be nearing eight-thirty. If I was fast.

And this time in the morning . . . I did some calculating of L.A. rush hour traffic and knew I needed to be fast if we were going to make it from Pierce and Artie's in Malibu to Temecula.

I spun for the bedroom.

"I'm going to shower really quick. Do you need me to rustle you up a change of clothes? I'm sure I can grab something of Pierce's from the house."

Talbot shook his head. "I've got my bag in my car. I'll shower when you're done."

He strode to the door. I headed for the bathroom.

"Oh, hey," I said just before I went inside. "What's the name of the winery?"

"Lakeland Lucha."

I froze. "Really?"

"Have you had it?"

I laughed. "Two bottles of their Chardonnay last night. It's good."

Talbot grinned. "That's why you took so long to answer the door."

"Shut it, you," I said with a glare, chuckling as I pushed into the bathroom. "Clothes. Shower. Successful business meeting."

He saluted as I shut the door and started up the water.

What were the odds that Talbot had a meeting at the winery whose variety I'd just downed like grape juice instead of alcohol the night before because it was so good?

Knowing the world was sometimes a strange, small place, I smiled and stepped into the hot water, taking the quickest shower on record, wrapping myself in a towel and leaving it running because Talbot had called out to me, letting me know he'd made it back inside and was waiting in the hall for his turn. Decent, I opened the door and hurried past him to the bedroom to get dressed.

Of course, if I'd known what was about to happen at the very winery we were headed to, I would have been a lot less sanguine.

I certainly wouldn't have been laughing as we rushed to the car thirty minutes later, giggling when Talbot jokingly called me a lush.

And I definitely wouldn't have been planning on buying a case of the Chardonnay.

Or maybe two.

But I didn't know what . . . or rather, *who* awaited me.

NINE

Aaron

I GLANCED AT MY PHONE, presumably to check the time since my important Hollywood client was nearing ten minutes late for our meeting. But, in reality, I was checking to see if Maggie had texted back.

Because I'd never expected my Hollywood client to be on time.

Because I was really hoping that Mags would have texted back.

I'd spent too long crafting a single sentence, probably a *pathetically* long time considering it had now been more than twelve hours without a response.

I was trying to figure out if I should send something else—something like, *Hey. It's Aaron. I was an ass and I'm sorry. Can we talk?*—when I saw the dust kicking up in the distance. A shiny black SUV maneuvered its way along the curving road that led up to the stone and wooden entrance of the vineyard.

We'd closed bookings to any tastings today, in deference to our guest's star power. Not that we'd had to turn people away, since it was a weekday and pretty damned early in the morning for drinking.

But apparently Talbot Green was a big name in town, and he and his girlfriend required privacy.

I glanced to my right, to the trio of managers from this branch of Lakeland Lucha, who oversaw everything day to day at our California location, as well as our marketing team, who were in charge of U.S. promotion. I was superfluous for this meeting, but it was important to Carlos that I be here to "feel" Talbot out.

I got it—in a monetary sense, rather than Carlos's bare feet wisdom. But the point was that we were going to spend a lot of marketing dollars on this deal, and it needed to be worth it.

I slipped my cell into my pocket just as the SUV pulled through the stone archway and navigated its way up to our little crowd of wine people.

It slid to a stop, the engine turned off, and the passenger door popped open.

I'd already walked over, readying to assist Talbot's girlfriend out of the car, when I heard it.

Laughter.

My laughter. Or rather, the laughter that was supposed to be meant for me, and *only* me.

Feet sliding to a stop, I watched a black slack-covered leg appear from behind the door then another. My gaze drew up, taking in the shapely hips, the waist I'd gripped too many times to count, the breasts that were more luscious now than they'd been a decade before. I saw a glimpse of golden skin in the V of her shirt. I took in the gleaming brown locks, a lush bottom lip, a rosebud top one. I counted the freckles on her left cheek—one, two, three, four. I—

Talbot and his *girlfriend.*

Fuck.

I was too late.

She was still laughing as she slid clear of the door, slamming the metal panel shut and turning to face me.

Maggie faltered, lips parting in surprise, eyes widening.

"Sweetheart," a man I presumed to be Talbot said as he came around the front of the SUV. "Is everything okay?"

Sweetheart. *Girlfriend.*

Fuck.

The man slid an arm over Maggie's shoulders, glanced down at her then up at me, expression curious. "Hi," he said, keeping his arm in place, but extending the other in my direction. "I'm Talbot. Nice to meet you."

Bile burned the back of my throat.

My mind was stuck in the perpetual cycle of *sweetheart, girlfriend, Maggie, Talbot.*

And *fuck.*

Because there were plenty of f-bombs floating around my brain as well. Enough that it took me several awkward seconds to lift my own hand and shake Talbot's.

"Aaron," I said. "Nice to meet you." I turned my gaze to Maggie. "Mags," I murmured, knowing that it was too late but wanting her to know that I'd finally got it, that I was growing up. I could be polite, even though it was killing me to see she was with another man.

I got that it had been ten years and clearly, she'd been with other people. But this was *Mags.* She was supposed to have been mine, and . . . she wasn't. But I could still be rational, could show her I'd moved past my anger, that her last words had had some effect.

"It's good to see you." A beat as I struggled to smother what came out next . . . and failed, obviously, because the next words that crossed my lips were, "I've missed you."

She gasped slightly, her cheeks blazing with pink even as

her chin lifted. "Good to see you," she said and stepped out from beneath Talbot's shoulder, heading over to the grouping of my employees huddled at the entrance to the cellar.

I watched her shoulders rise and fall on a deep inhale and slow exhale, knowing I was staring but unable to stop myself. The sun had gilded her skin. Those black slacks encased curves I'd once known intimately, and finally, *finally* I understood how much my anger had hidden.

Want.

I wanted.

Need.

I needed.

Desire.

I was aching with it.

And she was with someone else.

A man who cleared his throat, tugging my focus back to him and the fact that my hand was still wrapped around his.

I pulled back, cleared my throat. "Sorry." I sucked in a breath, forced my mind to stop racing and focused on what needed to happen. This meeting to go smoothly. Me to feel out this man. My team allowed the opportunity to give the presentation they'd worked so hard to prepare to a Hollywood celebrity. "Please, come over and we'll show you around."

"Thanks," he said, bleeping the locks on the SUV and walking alongside me. "You said your name was Aaron?"

I nodded. "Aaron Weaver. My business partner, Carlos, and I own this winery and a few others."

"I see." His eyes were on the horizon, feet slowing before we got too close to the rest of my employees. "And how do you know Maggie?"

A quietly probing question. One I would have asked if I were in his position.

"We grew up together."

"In Utah?"

I nodded again.

"Hmm."

Slow steps moving forward, slow enough they gave me the opportunity to ask, "How long have you and Maggie been together?"

"Three years."

Three. Years.

A total gut punch. I had thought I'd do some thinking and tell Mags I'd realized I had been an idiot, that I'd changed my mind and wanted to see what ten years of apart might bring us if we found a way back together. I'd thought she might not be receptive, and I knew that would have been my fault.

But I'd never considered that she might be with someone else.

Fuck.

"Talbot?" Maggie's voice penetrated the red haze of my spiraling mind and drew my focus like a laser beam.

But she wasn't looking at me.

I thought I might throw up.

"Yeah, babe?" Talbot said, closing the distance between them, heading over to Mags and slipping his arm around her again. She didn't react, didn't pull away, as I half-hoped.

Because they'd been together for three years. They were comfortable. They'd built something.

They'd built. I'd destroyed.

I hung back as introductions were made, as hands were shaken, as my managers began the tour, and I knew I was supposed to be evaluating Talbot, seeing if he'd fit with our brand and image, suss out Carlos's bare feet sensibilities, but my eyes didn't work for anyone but Maggie.

Three weeks, and I'd realized a critical truth.

But I was three *years* too late.

Someone opened the cellar door, and I knew the plan was that they'd lead the group down into the private tasting room, a space that was ensconced in a softly lit, cool-year-round corner of the bottom floor.

Wine would be served, paired with delectable treats from a menu that had been prepared for Talbot and his girlfriend by our talented on-site chef.

Then they'd proceed forward through the cellar, learn about the wine-making process before moving out into the hills to see our vines, dormant and naked of leaves during this time of year.

And . . . I just couldn't.

I. Couldn't.

Letting the door close, cutting me off from the rest of the group, I spun away and hauled ass out into the vineyard.

Then I did something I'd never thought I would do.

I sank to the dirt, pressed the bare skin of my palms to the earth, and I tried to ground myself in everything I'd built, everything Carlos and I had ahead of us.

I did everything I could to push away the past and to think of the future.

I did everything I could to focus on the rough dirt, the heat of the sun beating down on me, to feel the soft whisper of the wind against my skin.

I did everything I could to forget about the woman inside that private tasting room.

Everything wasn't enough.

Because I couldn't forget her, no matter how hard I tried.

TEN

Maggie

I SLIPPED AWAY from Talbot as he gushed over one of the tasty appetizers the winery's chef had prepared and tried to process what had happened not thirty minutes before.

What had happened. *Ha.*

I was trying to process Aaron.

Here.

In California. Two hours from me.

"You've met Aaron, our owner," Celeste, one of the marketing strategists for the winery I'd met outside had said when I left him and Talbot, mind spinning, trying to make sense of . . .

Why in the ever-loving fuck Aaron was in California.

Why he was apparently the owner of a winery in California when the Aaron I'd known hadn't even drank.

And being kids from a small town, kids with plenty of open spaces and safe streets to drunkenly make our way home, homes that were out in the middle of nowhere with nothing exciting going on . . . and our group of friends had perfected underaged drinking.

But not Aaron.

Never Aaron.

He'd driven us home. He'd held back hair as we'd christened the porcelain goddess and provided ibuprofen and water bottles for the rough wake-ups the following mornings, but he hadn't gotten drunk alongside us.

And now he owned a winery.

It made no sense.

None of this made any sense.

I drifted through the door as Talbot continued to munch and drink—my friend and client was never happier than while eating good food and drinking good wine. The opening led to a set of stairs leading down. Knowing that Tal would be otherwise occupied with the food and the winery's team for a while, I figured I might as well take a look around.

The staircase led to a narrow hallway, but instead of giving off creepy, ax murderer vibes, I was intrigued. Stone lined the walls, soft lights overhead made sure there weren't any scary shadows. And the hall was short, leading to another door, this one open and showing off a large space that was filled with huge wooden barrels.

I stepped through into the cellar that was more football field than home wine storage and spent a few moments gaping at the sheer volume.

"Incredible, isn't it?"

I jumped and whirled around, seeing a man with a Lakeland Lucha T-shirt, his dark hair peppered with gray, but his brown eyes filled with amusement.

"Sorry." His lips twitched.

My hand was over my heart, the organ having skipped a few beats due to the words that had surprised me out of my reverie.

"My fault," I told him. "I"—I waved a hand at the rows and rows of giant barrels—"just wow. I didn't expect it to be this *big*."

He lifted a brow.

I felt my cheeks heat as I processed my words and how they could be taken, but aside from that brow, his reply didn't let on that he'd caught the double entendre. Apparently, that was me and my issue. Cool. Another to add to the list. I was supposed to be good at words, at picking them carefully. That I'd somehow gone down the path of innuendos told me how much seeing Aaron had rattled my typically professional demeanor.

"I'm Maggie," I said, lifting my chin, pulling myself back into the present and the job I was supposed to be doing, and extending my hand.

"Harry." We shook then he tilted his head to the side, asked, his tone curious, "What *did* you expect?"

I let my gaze drift back to the barrels. "A small family operation, I guess."

A chuckle.

"Why did you laugh?" I asked, turning back.

His beard twitched when he smiled at me. "Only that Lakeland Lucha is global. Carlos and Aaron recently expanded the operation to Italy."

"Italy?" I gasped.

He nodded.

"Where else have they expanded?"

"The winery in France. Here. And they still have their original location in Utah."

"Utah?" I asked, gaping.

Another chuckle. "I know. Not the typical wine region, but Carlos has been growing a variety of ice wine there for a little more than a decade. The results over the last few seasons have really taken off, enabled Lakeland to grow."

"Wow," I said, eyeing the barrels again, wondering why I wanted to run my fingers over the rough-looking wood.

"We make Chardonnay here, though."

I grinned. "Not much ice in these parts."

"No," Harry said. "Can't say there is."

"I've had the Chardonnay from here," I told him. "I really enjoyed it."

"Glad to hear."

I bit my lip. "Is it okay if I look around?"

"Seeing as you're already doing it?" There, that brow lifted again. See? The innuendos were my issue. "I'm teasing," he said, no doubt because my face had paled, and I'd been trying to summon an excuse or apology to my tongue. "Look away." He waved a hand at the barrels. "The employee areas are marked with signs, so be sure to not enter those parts without an escort."

"Will the wine guards get me?" I teased back, starting to understand the mischief in the man's expression. It was hard to discern, but it was there.

Harry's beard twitched again. "No, but there is some machinery that can be dangerous. Unless you want me to give you a tour and explain the process of making wine?" That brow lifted once more.

I stifled a shudder, wanting to learn the process of wine-making about as much as I had wanted to learn about coding for arrays during my date last night.

Drinking wine? Yes. I was all about that.

Learning about the chemicals and fermentation and the notes of honey and oak Talbot had been waxing poetic about upstairs was why I'd gone off exploring on my own in the first place.

"Thanks for the offer . . ." I began.

"But not necessary." He picked up a clipboard with another

beard twitch. "Good. I have work to do. You'll avoid those Employee-Only areas?"

I nodded. "Employee areas. Avoided. Check." Another nod, but then I paused, asked, "Is it an issue if I go look at the vines?"

Harry shook his head. "No," he said. "Though, they're not much to look at this time of year. Still, feel free to walk the hills if you want. There's a door on the other side of the cellar. You might not see any grapes, but you'd be in for a nice view."

"A nice view sounds perfect." I smiled. "Thanks."

"Yup."

He slipped out into the hall, and I spent the next few minutes making my way through the barrels. God, they were huge. Twice as tall as me and sitting on racks that looked far too spindly to support them. I kept having to blink away the image of one after another of the stands collapsing, the barrels tipping to the side, wine bursting out and filling the space—

Making a wine swimming pool.

Hmm. I could get behind that.

Giggling to myself, I kept walking. I spied the door on the opposite end of the space that was marked overhead with an exit sign and pushed through.

Then had to bite back another gasp.

I'd expected more stairs leading up, but instead, this door led to the outside, to a blindingly bright panoramic view of the vineyard.

"Oh, wow," I murmured. The only thing that was green were some strips of vegetation between the vines, the grapes and leaves having been pruned back to the brown stalks of the plants themselves. The sun was high overhead, the sky blue and cloudless . . . and it was quiet.

No traffic noise. No smog.

Just the soft whisper of the wind, the warmth of the sun shining down.

I closed my eyes and stayed frozen for a long moment, feeling the solidness of the earth beneath, the breeze teasing the ends of my hair. I'd moved from Utah because I'd wanted to experience more of the outside world, to see big things, to live my life to the fullest.

But that didn't mean I couldn't appreciate this.

Nature. Rays of sunlight coating my skin, the whistle of the wind as it flowed through the vines, even the smell of the dirt. It was so similar to my father's ranch in Utah, so much like the environment I'd grown up in.

In a way, being able to ground myself in this way felt like . . . home.

Would *always* be home.

The softest scuff of a shoe had my eyes sliding open, blinking against the bright, knowing who would be there even before I saw Aaron standing before me.

I'd known it was him, and still my heart skipped a beat.

I'd known it was him, and *still* I felt a flash of heat down my spine.

I worked in Hollywood. I worked with clients who had stylists and personal trainers, private chefs and hair and makeup people . . . and Aaron was still the most gorgeous man I'd ever laid eyes on.

He didn't say anything, just stared at me for a long, long time.

I held my breath, waited for the sharp edge of his anger, more harsh words like our last phone conversation, like we'd exchanged in my father's kitchen.

Lungs burning, I forced myself to suck in air. Slowly, as though I were avoiding a predator who might pounce at any moment—and Aaron had proven to me a month ago that even though a decade had gone by, he still was absolutely capable of turning that razor-like blade of his anger on me—I slid back a step.

"Don't," he said, voice intense, almost heavy with emotion.

But I'd already stopped myself, forced my feet to stay in place.

I wouldn't accept his anger.

Absolutely not.

Ten years had gone by. He needed to shut up and get over it, and we could move forward as two polite, mature adults. I shored up my courage, parted my lips to congratulate him on the sheer scope of his business—

"I'm sorry."

My jaw dropped open.

He took a step toward me, stopped then thrust a hand through his hair. "I'm so damned sorry, Mags. I—" Aaron broke off, paced away.

When more words didn't come, I found myself asking, "Why? Why now?"

I watched him walk a few more steps away, reveled in the lines of his shoulders, broader now than when we'd been in our teens, exulted in the leanness of his waist, the power of his legs. He'd grown taller, filled out, and yet, he was still Aaron.

I could have picked him out from a mile away. Or maybe that was just because my body was still so in tune with his.

He was near; I was drawn in.

Like planets around the sun.

Aaron was mine.

That was why I'd needed to go. Because if I hadn't left ten years ago, if I hadn't cobbled together the strength to leave him behind, I *never* would have left. Maybe we'd have a family, a house, a white picket fence, but I knew I would never be completely fulfilled, never have *this* life I'd built. And Aaron—

He spun to face me, and I was momentarily frozen in place

by the sheer breadth of emotion traveling through his expression.

Regret. Pain. Despair. Loneliness.

Each one was an impact against my gut, my mind, my . . . heart.

Footsteps echoed across the paved path, signaling he was coming closer, but I was still reeling from the brunt of his emotions, aching from the need to soothe. Gentle hands picked mine up, held them like they were the most fragile piece of crystal on Earth.

"I want to have a good answer for you," he said, voice rasping along my nape, my spine. "I want to tell you I had this huge ah-ha moment where suddenly everything you said ten years ago, everything you said a month ago, hit me like a load of bricks."

My throat was tight. "But?"

"But that would be a lie." His fingers brushed my wrists, tracing little patterns that had goose bumps lifting on my skin. "I was furious when you left. So pissed you were leaving again after you'd gone a decade ago that I couldn't begin to even process your words." Another brush before his thumb and forefinger circled the oval of my wrist. "Until I was alone in the quiet bunkhouse."

I bit my lip, not knowing what to say.

Luckily, I didn't need to come up with anything, because he continued talking. "I think it was just easier for me to pretend you were the bad guy in leaving than to admit that I'd played a role."

"I—"

"No, Peaches," he whispered. "Will you let me say this?"

I inhaled rapidly at the nickname then slowly released the air. "Okay."

"It was a blow to my ego, for sure. That you managed to

leave when it was impossible for me to want to let you go. Except . . . it wasn't impossible," he said, "was it? If I'd really loved you then like I should have, I would have come after you. I would have barreled my way back into your life and never let go, no matter what state you were living in."

"Your mom got sick," I said, shaking my head. "You couldn't have . . ." I bit my lip, letting the words trail off as I remembered his fury the last time I'd brought up his mother.

But the fury didn't come.

Instead, if anything, his shoulders relaxed infinitesimally. "My mom would have still gotten sick whether I was here or back in Utah."

"And college?" I pointed out. "You had been accepted to school at home."

His hands slipped from mine, sad creeping into his oaky brown eyes. "I didn't even try for a college in SoCal. I was so inflexible in my thinking that I just assumed I'd be able to bully or cajole or pressure you into staying." A firm shake of his head. "That wasn't right. It wasn't okay. Just like it wasn't right or okay to be furious with you, to blame you for everything that didn't work out in my life for ten years. I was inflexible and immature and didn't take any ownership for my part of our breakup."

I smiled. "Aar, we were *eighteen*," I said. "I don't think taking ownership is in our DNA at that age, let alone flexibility. I wanted what I wanted, and I wasn't going to change my mind."

"Pot. Meet kettle."

My lips twitched. "Yeah," I murmured. "We had stubborn down."

"It was easier to be mad than to accept I missed you but was too damned scared to come after you."

Breath catching, I studied this man's face. So familiar to the Aaron of the past, and yet so different. Soft, thoughtful words instead of anger and resentment. Aaron of my past had been wonderful. Caring and sweet, but his stubborn had been edged with mean.

Like my dad.

Except . . . when had my dad ever looked into my eyes and apologized? For anything big or small?

That would be . . . never.

"Why do you stay on the ranch?"

"I thought it was to look after your old man." He made a face. "My attempt at martyrdom in taking care of something that reinforced my right to be pissed at you. Shirking your responsibilities, not showing up when you should." I winced and he caught it, closing the distance between us, cupping my face between slightly roughened palms. "No, Peaches. That's not the point. Because you *didn't* do that. You came home for his birthday, for Christmas. You took care of him for as long as he would let you after the heart attacks, paid for nurses he couldn't afford—Claudette is great and the only person I've ever seen to get your father on his back foot, by the way—"

I chuckled. "She is."

"You were there for your family in a way he wasn't there for you."

My gaze darted to the side, and I stepped back. "That's— He's—" I shook my head. "I've accepted that sometimes the people in your life are just unable to be there for you in the way you crave and that focusing on it, wishing things were different, doesn't change anything."

"That's bullshit."

I gaped.

"Sorry, but it is. Your dad is as bad as me. Blaming you for something that wasn't your fault. Your mom died." I inhaled shakily, and he came to me, placed his hand on the side of my neck. "It wasn't anyone's fault. Bad things happen, but you needed him, and he let the anger of losing her eat through him." His chest rose and fell on a long breath. "I was the same, and I'm sorry I didn't understand, didn't fight for you like I should have. And I'm so fucking sorry I didn't recognize any of this sooner."

Pulse pounding, I covered his hand with mine. "A-aaron," I whispered.

He rested his forehead against mine. "I can't believe I missed out on all these years because of it, and I can't believe I'm going to keep missing out because you're with someone who looks at you right."

My brows drew down and I pulled back slightly, enough to see his eyes, but not far enough to dislodge the warmth of his palm. Not when it felt so good to have his hand there.

And no, I wasn't digesting *that* too closely.

Physical connection and chemistry hadn't been our issue . . . it was just everything else that had gone to hell.

Anyway, my brain was focused on his touch, but it was also struggling to process everything he'd said. Which is probably why I just blurted, "I'm not with someone."

His eyes widened. "What?"

"I'm single."

"What about Talbot?"

Yes, I heard the slight note of jealousy in his voice. Yes, I felt that gruff note slide down between my thighs.

I shouldn't have cared.

I should have been thankful for the apology, glad to be able to put a painful piece of my past behind me.

And I was . . . I just also wasn't sure if I was quite ready to put *Aaron* behind me.

Behind. Me.

Dear Lord.

The skin over my cheeks went hot, and with our faces so close together, Aaron didn't miss the flush, and there was no way he could miss my breath shuddering out on a long, slow exhale when I thought of *this* Aaron, strong and kind, who was touching me gently, who'd apologized, whose broad chest was so near mine, taking me from behind.

Physical. Emotional.

Everything was tangled up together.

"Why are you blushing?"

Yeah, that wasn't something I was prepared to share with the class.

"Talbot is my client, not my boyfriend," I explained instead.

"Client?" More brows drawing together, forming a little V I wanted to smooth away with my fingers.

I nodded.

His fingers flexed beneath mine, but I didn't drop my hand. Stupid? Probably, and yet, I wasn't quite ready to break the connection.

"My team said he was coming with his girlfriend."

"That was initially the plan," I said. "But things . . . well, there was an issue and Kelsey couldn't come."

"An issue."

Since I'd nearly blown it and given away something private of Talbot's—a huge no-no in my line of work, I just nodded.

"Hmm." A considering pause. "So, you're saying you're single."

Finally, I dropped my hand, stepped back, nerves ramping at that simple statement. "Yes?" And it was definitely more question than statement.

Aaron smiled, wide and bright and so much like the Aaron of ten years ago that I nearly gasped aloud. "Good, so then you'll go to dinner with me?"

"That's not—" I shook my head. "I don't think—"

"Don't," he murmured, coming close again, the spicy scent of man washing over me, his hand coming to my wrist again, but instead of stroking patterns on my skin, I felt something cool and metal brushing against me, rough fingers fumbling for a moment. He lifted my arm, and my pulse sped when I saw what he'd put on my wrist.

My bracelet.

No longer bright and shiny and new.

But back on my wrist anyway.

He leaned close, hot breath in my ear, and whispered, "Don't think, Peaches. Just feel."

Except, I couldn't *just feel*, not when what was between us had been an aching hole in my heart for years. Not when his apology, his gentle words were still swirling through my brain, trying to make sense of everything he'd just dropped right out in the open.

"Aaron," I murmured, still shaking my head.

He brushed his fingers over my cheek. "My mom told me you'd kept in touch with her."

I felt my eyes widen.

"She told me that she suggested you stay away."

I let my eyes drift to the hills again, to the brown vines, focused on the feel of the wind on my skin, the bright blue sky. "It was the right call."

"I know," he murmured. "She also told me to use my powers for good." A beat. "Right before she told me to call you." His expression went self-deprecating. "Instead, I texted."

I frowned, remembered the weird message from the unknown number. "That was you?"

"Yes," he said on a wince. "I know it wasn't smooth, but now that I've apologized via text and now in person, will you let me complete the trifecta and do it over dinner?"

I shouldn't.

But as I stared into his eyes, a deep, rich brown with flecks of gold, I knew that I wasn't going to say no, either.

Accepting the inevitable, I leaned closer, let my chest come very near his. "If I say yes . . . are you going to explain the function of finding the largest number in an array for me?"

His gaze had gone hot—until the last bit of my sentence. Then confusion shone.

"I'll explain anything you want," he said. "So long as you let me take you out to dinner."

I grinned, stepped back so that his hand fell away. "Then you'd better find a math textbook," I teased, "because you have some studying up to do."

He tugged a strand of my hair. "Is that a yes?"

Just live.

Could I? *Should* I?

Hell, it was my freaking mantra. How could I not?

I nibbled at the corner of my mouth. "It's a yes."

Another grin that stole my breath, one more brush of knuckles over my cheek that seared my every nerve ending. "I'll pick you up at seven, Peaches."

ELEVEN

Aaron

I SHOVED MY HAND, its palm burning from the contact with Mag's skin, into my pocket when I heard voices coming around the corner, stepping back from Maggie and turning to face the group as they continued their tour.

Talbot was nodding and smiling, but his eyes were on mine, and he lifted a brow.

Probably because Mags had her back to the group.

"You okay?" I asked softly.

A nod, her chin coming up, her shoulders straightening,

I'd seen her do that so many times that witnessing it in this moment was comfortable, almost nostalgic.

She turned, tagged his head of marketing, Jesse, with a look, and then pulled the other woman into a conversation about social media presence. Two seconds later, they were off and running, words like branding, audience demographics, and targeting making me tune out.

Give me spreadsheets any day of the week.

Plus, I had a bone to pick with Talbot.

"You've been together for three years?" I asked when he approached. The man was way too pretty, and he knew it, based on the confident smile he slid my way upon being trapped in a lie.

"I said together." A shrug. "But I never said in what way."

An equivocation then.

"Hmm," I muttered. "So, you've worked together for three years."

"She took a chance on me," he said. "Because of her and her connections, her stubbornness, really"—another award-winning smile here—"she helped me get my big break with Artie's company. So, when she wanted to branch out, to get into publicity and start her own business, I stuck with her." A shrug. "Just like she stuck with me."

"You two are close."

"Yes." Gold eyes narrowed. "You hurt her."

Guilt.

Fuck, it was a heavy feeling.

"I made a mistake," I said.

"A mistake?" Talbot's tone was deadly.

I bristled, even knowing I deserved the derision. "Look, I was a selfish prick," I said. "I wronged her, horribly, but I don't owe you any apology or restitution. That, I'm saving for her."

Respect on the other man's face. "And have you?" he asked. "Have you apologized?"

"Not that it's any of your business—"

"It is." No negotiation in his tone.

"—but, yes. I've apologized," I went on, ignoring the interruption. I hated that this stranger was trying to take me to task, but I could get beyond that, was glad that Mags had someone on her side. Someone who'd have her back. She needed that. "I've apologized," I said. "And I'll keep doing so for as long as it takes for her to forgive me, for me to make it up to her. I'll continue to apologize forever because she'd didn't deserve the shit I shoveled her way." I inhaled, swallowed hard. "I fucking failed her, and I will *not* do it again."

Silence for a long, drawn-out moment.

"See that you don't." Then he nodded, face clearing, award-winning smile peeking back out. "Now that's out of the way, do you know how I can score myself some bottles of wine?"

"Are you going to be the face of Lakeside Lucha?" Not only did I know that Carlos would love Talbot, but I was also confident he'd be up to the task of promoting our company because he was Maggie's client. And that was enough vouching for me. He nodded and I grinned despite myself. "Then I think I might be able to arrange for some complimentary bottles."

I RANG the buzzer in front of a forbidding gate later that evening, my mouth dropping open as I took in the house and grounds beyond.

Apparently, the PR thing paid good money, if the size of this mansion was any indication.

The gate swung open, and I pulled my car through, parking in front of a three-car garage and eyeing the large double front doors, all mahogany wood and iron, wondering not for the first time since I'd watched Mags drive off with Talbot, if I was in over my head.

But before I could work up any sincere worry, I saw legs.

A physical shake, a mental push to get my brain to focus.

Except, that had the effect of drawing my gaze up those shapely legs, taking in the sight of Maggie's short and sexy dress, its hemline flirting at mid-thigh and threatening to drive me insane in the sum total of three seconds since I'd laid eyes on her.

And maybe math was in my head because I'd looked up what an array was after she'd left, or more likely because I'd spent this afternoon and evening adding up all of the ways I could get her back into my life, summing them together and hoping and praying that the total would be enough to convince her to give me another shot.

Dinner.

I needed to start with dinner first.

Shoving open my door, I hurried to meet up with her. "Mags," I said, my eyes taking in the rest of her dress—tight on the curves of her hips, snug enough over her breasts to snag my gaze there for several seconds before I managed to not be a total pig and wrench my stare to her face.

Her hair was down. Her makeup was pristine. Her lips . . . they were coated in bright red, and curving up in a sinful, confident female smirk that sent heat arrowing toward my cock.

Holy hell.

"Hi," she murmured.

"Nice house," I blurted, too loud, to staccato, and not slick or refined in any way, shape, or form. I immediately cursed myself. Acting the part of a bumbling young idiot wasn't part of my plan to show Mags I'd changed, that things were different.

But instead of teasing me for my abruptness, she just smiled. "This is Pierce and Artie's place." A shrug. "Paying for my dad's care meant my plan to save for a down payment for a house got a bit derailed. I actually live in the guest house out back," she told me. "Luckily, I have some cool clients."

"They're lucky to have you, too."

She smiled. "You don't have to be charming."

A thread of stubborn wove through me. "I'm not being charming," I said. "I don't think you'd have four of the biggest clients in the world without being good at your job."

Mags tucked a strand of hair behind her ear. "Did you spend the afternoon researching my clients?"

I laced my fingers with hers, started moving her in the direction of my car. "Well, I certainly didn't spend the *whole* time studying arrays."

She giggled then stopped, heels clicking to a halt on the driveway. "Wait. Did you really study what an array is?"

I lifted a brow. "An array is a data structure made up of a collection of elements, each of which is identified by at least one key, also known as an array index."

Mags blinked, started walking again. "Wow. I think my mind just froze over."

"Hey!" I nudged her lightly with my shoulder. "You're the one who wanted to know," I said. "I learned much more about data processing than I wanted to this afternoon."

She grinned. "You really want to do this, don't you?"

My hand had been reaching for the passenger door, readying to open it for her, but her question made me stop and look at her. "What do you mean?"

"I—" She shrugged, started to reach for the handle herself. "Never mind. It doesn't matter."

The hell it didn't.

"Mags," I said, stepping closer, pinning her between the car and my body.

Her hands lifted like she was going to push me away. I would have let her, of course, would have stepped back if she asked, if she nudged me back, but since she didn't, since her hands fluttered in the air for a moment before settling onto my chest, the touch a hot brand of sensation, I didn't retreat.

I stayed in place, motionless, the scent of her totally overwhelming my senses.

Her mouth opened, a shaking exhale glazing my lips like the

sweet peach preserves our town was famous for in the summer months.

Her fingertips were hot brands, soaking through the cotton of my button-down.

"Let's go to dinner," she breathed.

I nodded . . . and look at that, my mouth was near the lusciousness of her bare shoulder, her throat, her exposed collar bones. Inhaling, I nuzzled at the spot where her neck met her chest, breathing in her sweet smell, letting it wash over me completely. "Yes," I murmured. "Let's go to dinner."

But neither of us moved.

We stayed in place, bodies inches apart, breathing in the other's exhalations, warmth spreading and growing the longer we remained close.

My lips pressed lightly to her throat, to her jaw, to the spot just beneath it that had always made her shiver. "What did you mean, Peaches?"

"Hmm?" she asked, hands slipping up from my chest, sliding around to the back of my neck, up into my hair.

"Earlier, when you asked if I really wanted to do this."

She froze, dropped her hands, chocolate eyes drifting from mine to over my left shoulder.

"I just—" A sigh, and now her hands pressed at my chest.

I stepped back. Not far. But back a pace or two. "Peaches."

Her eyes flashed to mine then away again. "I can't believe you remember that stupid nickname."

"I had wet dreams for years after that time in the orchard."

Cheeks flaring pink, she gaped at me. "Aaron! You can't say that."

Closer again, not touching but near enough to soothe the burn of my need to be in her proximity, to smell, to listen to the slight increase in her breathing when I did so. "Why not?"

"Because we're past wet dreams and old memories."

"I will never forget the first time you let me make out with you, tasting the juice of the peaches we'd stolen on your lips, your sticky fingers winding into my hair." I grinned, despite myself. "I swear, I didn't shower for four days, just so I could keep the scent of you in my pores."

"I-I didn't know," she whispered.

"I should have told you," I murmured. "Should have realized how important you were, should have made you see that, too. Maybe then things would have . . ."

Silence.

Then fingers on my cheek. "You don't know it would have made a difference."

"I know it would have changed things between us now," I said. "And speaking of now, *what did you mean?*"

To her credit, she didn't back down or immediately give in. But that was my Mags, wasn't it? Strong to her core. A stubborn streak a mile wide. Smart and tough and . . . mine.

Now, I just had to convince *her* of that.

A mulish expression pulled her lips flat, wrinkled her nose, and . . . *I* gave in.

To her hands curling into my shirt. To the growing need between us. To the present and the past and the possibility of a future.

I dropped my head, slanted my lips across hers.

It was . . . coming home.

That was the only way to describe her mouth against mine, the way her hands slid back up my neck, threading into my hair again without hesitation. She tipped forward on the sexy as shit heels, breasts coming to press against my chest, and her lips opened, tongue sliding against mine.

A kiss we'd done a hundred, a thousand times.

And yet, a kiss that was different. Deeper. Stronger. More.

Mine, my brain blared again, releasing the hold on my

control, my hands coming up to her face, cupping her cheeks in my palms, angling her head so her lips were flush against mine, so I could taste her more fully.

Still sweet. Still earnest. Still the absolute best kiss of my life.

She pushed back slightly, tearing her mouth away, sucking in air in rapid gusts. "Holy . . . shit," she panted. "That . . . was —" A shake of her head, fingers coming to her lips. "I'd thought that I'd made this"—a wave of those fingers between us—"chemistry out to be more than it was."

"No," I said, and it was more growl than disagreement.

For some reason, that made her smile, rub her jaw against mine, soft words in my ear. "Earlier . . . I'd thought this, that you wanting to take me for dinner, was mostly out of guilt."

Fury tore through me and I lurched back, lips parting, readying to disabuse her of that notion. But then *she* kissed *me*, cutting off the words, thrusting her tongue into my mouth, pressing her body to mine, and making me see stars from the intensity of the contact.

"I get now I was wrong," she said against my lips when we broke apart for air.

"I—"

Another kiss, leaving me rock-hard, hands clenched into fists where they rested on her hips.

She gave me another little shove, nudging me back, tugging open the passenger door before I got my brain together enough to do it. Sinking into the seat in a move that sent the skirt of her dress scandalously, *temptingly* high, she blew me a kiss.

"Let's go to dinner, baby," she ordered.

Then she tugged the door closed, leaving me no choice but to follow orders.

Luckily, that was an easy one to obey.

TWELVE

Maggie

HOW DID a non-drinker get into the wine industry?" I asked as we sat on opposite sides of a small round table overlooking the ocean.

That he'd taken me to this restaurant, a tiny hole-in-the-wall place known for fish tacos and margaritas, had pleased me to no end. He'd remembered my love of tacos—and apparently, I was still on the innuendo trend today because that made my mind giggle like a teenager—but more importantly, he'd chosen someplace not too fancy, with a gorgeous view, and quiet, so we could talk.

He'd been deliberate in his choice. Thoughtful.

Of course, I couldn't know his intentions because I didn't have the ability to read his mind. But if I thought of the boy from high school, the one who'd been the designated driver, who'd left ibuprofen and bottles of water on my nightstand, who'd lifted me onto his shoulders so I could pick the peach that was just out of reach, then yes, I could think he'd been deliberate in his choice. And if I thought of the man who'd held on to anger for a long time, but after my words had spent many hours pondering his reaction and finding room to grow, then, also yes, I could definitely imagine that boy who'd turned into *this* man being that thoughtful.

It was a mouthful . . . or rather a *mind*ful, but thankfully Aaron tugged me out of the maelstrom in my brain and back into the present.

"What makes you think I don't drink?"

I tilted my head to the side, eyes going from his water glass to my margarita.

The ghost of a smile. "I still can't stand tequila."

Chuckling, I allowed my eyes to go to the horizon, darkened to shades of navy and gray and black now that the sun had set. "I'd forgotten about that," I murmured. "I should amend my statement to: how does a one-time drinker own a winery?"

"It started with a summer job and an eccentric Italian, who decided to grow something called ice wine."

My brows drew down. "Well, our little slice of Utah *does* have plenty of ice in the winter months." I set my drink down and picked up my fork, scooping up a bit of lettuce and flaky whitefish that had fallen out of the tortilla. "But I always imagined that wine had to be grown in warm places." I made a face. "I guess I didn't really think that through, did I? France gets cold in the winter."

"That's true." He nodded. "Ice wine isn't common to Utah. Hell, wine in the first place isn't common in Utah. But Carlos had grown up in a wine family, and he was determined to experiment."

"Experiment how?"

"With the types of grapes," he said. "Chardonnay grapes aren't traditionally used in ice wine, but he wanted to try."

"And did it work?"

He grinned. "At first? No. It was a disaster. It takes about three years for vines to bear fruit, so there's no income off the vines for that length of time. Plus, sometimes it takes several more years beyond that to produce a good vintage." His eyes danced. "And ice wine, in particular, is finicky. You have to time the picking right, when the grapes are totally frozen, but the sugars inside are not. You have to rely on the weather, on hoping and praying they'll freeze fully before they rot on the vine."

"This might be a silly question," I said, taking a sip of my drink and thinking that wine speak was a lot more interesting than arrays. To each their own, I supposed. "But why can't you pick the grapes and pop them in a giant freezer?"

He laughed. "Not silly. You're right, but it wouldn't be ice wine. There are regulations governing the temperature at which they need to be fully frozen in order to have the name."

"That's crazy!" I exclaimed.

"That's the business," he said with a shrug.

A blip of guilt slid through me and I reached across the table, covering his hand with mine. "Sorry," I said. "I didn't mean to discount anything you've worked for." My tone went self-deprecating. "I'm just shocked that there's this whole world of wine I didn't know anything about."

"Something of an expert, are you?" he asked, one brow lifting.

I buffed my nails on my shoulder, blew on them. "I take my wine expert status seriously."

"Good to know." He flipped his palm over, capturing my fingers in his. "I didn't think you were trying to discount anything, Peaches," he added softly, thumb lightly tracing over the back of my knuckles.

The simple touch had heat shooting up my arm.

Probably a result of the margarita. They always went right through me.

But even as I tried to justify that in my brain, I knew that it had nothing to do with the tequila and everything to do with Aaron.

"Tell me more about your business," I said.

"Sure you wouldn't rather hear about arrays?"

I scowled and he chuckled, squeezing my hand lightly in the process.

"I'll give you the Cliffs Notes version because Carlos is really the visionary. I'm the numbers and facilities and spreadsheets guy."

"Not more numbers," I groaned.

A flash of white. "My work life is definitely all about the numbers, and the numbers are why we've focused on expanding our operations. Did you know that our ice wine grapes have to be picked at a moment's notice, sometimes in as little as a few hours?"

I shook my head.

"And the conditions are tough. Our team often picks overnight or in the early morning, and the pressing takes place in unheated spaces, for obvious reasons." He stopped, expression trending toward chagrinned. "Sorry, I'm blabbering on. Tell me about your—"

I squeezed his hand. "No, Aaron. This is fascinating. Tell me more."

"Mags," he said. "You can't possibly be fascinated by wine production."

Except, I was. Because this was Aaron and he was passionate about something, and I found I wanted to know every detail he did. Not processing that too deeply, I just squeezed his hand again when he hesitated, and said, "I'm guessing everything has to be done in the cold in order for the grapes to not unfreeze? What else?"

The cutest little furrow appeared between his brows. "Um . . . the fermentation process takes longer than a normal wine—

months compared to days and weeks."

"Wow. That seems like a lot of work."

He nodded. "It is. But the wine is very sweet and because it's such a risky and time-consuming process, the product also fetches top dollar."

"I can imagine," I said, lifting my glass with my free hand and polishing off my margarita. "I've never had ice wine. What does it taste like?"

"Very sweet, but not cloying. There's an acidity to it that makes it refreshing instead of overpowering." He used his free hand to tuck a strand of my hair behind my ear, and I had to say that I preferred his use of free hands touching me—to mine—drinking. "So," he asked, golden-brown eyes warm on mine. "Have I finally bored you with the wine speak?"

I found everything he was telling me utterly enthralling, not the least of which was how this man, who'd been so sure he wanted to be working a nine-to-five job in a small town in Utah, had ended up with an apparently global wine operation. "No. I have more questions," I told him. "Namely, how did you go from ice wine to vineyards in California, France, and Italy?" His brows lifted, and I shrugged, admitted, "I might have met a man named Harry in the cellar who gave me inside information."

Aaron snorted, but his lips twitched. "If anyone else said that grouping of words, I swear, I would have thought they were trying to pull a fast one."

"Is it the *man named Harry* part?" I teased. "Or the *in the cellar who gave me inside information* piece?"

"Neither. *Both.*" His face went serious as he put his free hand skills to good use again, this time cupping my cheek, the slightly roughened callouses on his palm sensitizing my skin. "God, I've missed you."

I'd missed him, too.

But part of me was still cautious. This man had hurt me

once. Oh, I knew *I'd* hurt *him*, too, that our breakup had been a slicing agony for both of us. Because of that I'd punished myself, felt guilty, harbored regrets. Aaron . . . he'd been angry. He hadn't sifted through the other emotions on and off for ten years like I had, and I was worried that his anger would flare again, and that I'd be on the receiving end of it once more.

Because I'd spent the last month thinking, too.

I'd spent the last month recovering from the interactions with my dad and with Aaron.

I wasn't going to be a punching bag any longer. I *couldn't* keep doing that.

No, I wasn't going to abandon my dad. My conscience wouldn't allow me to do that. I'd make sure to keep Claudette employed, ensure that the ranch was safe for him to live, but I wasn't going to continue to put myself through abuse just because I still felt guilty for leaving.

Emotionally, my dad had left me a long time ago. I'd needed and deserved so much more than I'd gotten.

I was done martyring myself, trying to fulfill those needs and desires with him.

Aaron's fingers convulsed lightly, his fingertips brushing my jaw. "I know that trust is earned, Peaches," he murmured.

I nodded, somehow unsurprised he'd been able to read my thoughts. "It is."

His thumb lightly traced my skin, back and forth, back and forth. "Can we just start with dinner?"

I wanted that.

I wanted more.

I *wanted* with an intensity that made me more than a little uneasy, that had me leaning back, slipping free of his hold, my skin highly sensitized from the contact, and turning to stare out at the ocean. Too dark to make out much more than the squiggle of the horizon, especially with the strands of lights winding overhead, impacting my night vision. But I wasn't focused so much on trying to see something as I was on what was going on in my mind, my heart.

Terrifying.

Sitting next to him, smelling him, *touching* him was scary.

Because I'd missed this. Because *this*—dinner, touching, bantering—was never quite as comfortable with another man.

But was that all it was? Comfortable? A familiar echo from the past?

Unable to keep my gaze on the ocean, my eyes found their way back to Aaron. He was watching me, patient expression on his face, and I knew, I *knew* that this wasn't just comfort.

Just live.

The whisper of a thought. One that had driven me to these shores, pushed me to keep going when I was hurt or sad or scared.

Just. Live.

I stared into Aaron's eyes, trying to ferret out every thought, desire, and fear in his soul, his mind, his body. And I found it in the perfectly calm expression, could see him war with himself to not say anything further, not wanting to influence my decision, even though I could tell he wanted me to say yes. It was there in the slight stiffness of his shoulders, in the tight corners of his mouth, in the careful way he held himself.

I could hurt him.

He was that open.

But I didn't want to hurt Aaron. I'd *never* wanted to hurt him, and the central core of me that had never fully let go of what we'd had, what had once been so great, didn't want to either.

That part of me wanted dinner. It wanted more. It—

Just. Live.

It wanted to forget about the past, about the things that were irrevocably broken, about all the ways we'd hurt each other.

It wanted to live.

But could I find the courage to make that leap?

I considered for a half-second before giving an inner snort. Could I find the courage? Fuck, yes. I could. I *always* found the courage to push forward. It was what made me so good at my job.

Now, I just needed to focus that courage on my personal life.

And I knew I could find the mettle to do that, too.

I shifted in my seat, fully facing him, and said, "We've already had dinner." His face started to fall, but I refused to let it go there, refused to allow him to be hurt again. Not when we had so much potential. I slid closer, ran my hand up his arm, leaned close. "How about we take a walk on the beach instead?"

He was frozen for a single heartbeat.

Then he paid the bill in record time, took my hand, and led me down the wooden steps that would carry us to the beach below.

"YOU NEVER TOLD me how you ended up with an international business when you'd planned on staying in Utah forever," I said, resting one hand on his shoulder as I used the other to slip off my heels.

Sand necessitated me breaking my *never remove my heels* rule, since I didn't relish sinking up to my ankles with every step. Or the likelihood of breaking one while trying to navigate sand in four-inch heels.

"It's a boring story," he said, his palms dropping to my waist to steady me when I switched feet. There was no denying that I enjoyed him touching me there, that I wanted our bodies to be closer . . . *naked* and closer.

"I revel in boring stories," I joked.

His teeth flashed, a glimpse of white in the dark sky. "Ice wine was risky to base our income on. When we had enough capital, I suggested the winery in Temecula. It grew Chardonnay, too, which Carlos was already familiar with, and it had a small, but stable crop, with a family looking to sell. The expansion made sense."

"More spreadsheets?" I asked, starting to hook my fingers into the straps of my heels.

Aaron snagged them from me then took my hand, tugging me out onto the sand. "More like cost analysis and risk-benefit ratios."

"Boring business stuff."

He shrugged. "It's my job, and I like the boring stuff."

"That's because you're a smarty-pants." I grinned, leaned my side against him as we walked between several large rocks on the beach, their sheer size lending some privacy in such a public place. Not that the beach was crowded at this time of night, but I liked the way the stones sheltered, how they muffled the crashing of the waves, made it seem like it was just Aaron and me in the world.

"Smarty-pants?" he asked.

I lifted my hands in a scale-like gesture, tone light. "And here I always thought I wanted to date someone pretty but dumb, so I didn't have to cross mental swords with him," I teased, shifting to glance up at him, my breast accidentally brushing his arm when I moved. My breath caught, but I continued the joke anyway. "Yet somehow, I stumbled onto pretty *and* smart." I tapped my chin. "What am I going to do with you, Aaron Weaver?"

He moved so fast that I didn't even have time for my breath to catch.

One second he was looking down at me, lips curved at the corners, head shaking at my silliness. The next, his mouth was on mine.

I gasped at the sheer volume of heat that exploded at the contact. It seared through my nerve endings, arrowing toward my nipples, my pussy. Then his tongue slipped inside, and I melted against him, letting the waves of pleasure lap at my body —warm, warmer, warmest, scalding, *inferno*.

Rough fingers on the backs of my thighs, teasing under the short skirt of my dress.

I broke away on a moan, those fingers sliding back and forth, dipping up, feeding that inferno with need and desire until it felt as though I might combust.

That was when Aaron set me away from him.

I wavered for a moment, and he steadied me as I found my feet, my body on fire. Then when I was stable, he bent and scooped up my heels, which he had apparently dropped to the sand. "Let's walk before I ignore my better judgment and take you on this beach."

My glance went to one of the rocks. It was the perfect height to perch me atop it, to slide my panties to the side, lift my skirt, and—

Another kiss that left me trembling and shaking.

"Not fair, Peaches."

I leaned heavily against him, trying to ignore the fact that I was seriously contemplating if our difference in height would make it possible for him to spin me around, to press my front to the tallest rock, and take me from behind. Or maybe he could lift me, and I'd wrap my legs around his waist.

There were so many possibilities.

I wanted to try them all.

"It's dark enough that I can't see your eyes clearly," he whispered, voice husky. "So, I shouldn't know all you're thinking."

I wrapped my arms around his shoulders. "Except you're thinking the same thing," I whispered back.

A flash of white, a nip on my nose, my bottom lip, my jaw.

"Yeah, Peaches. I'm thinking of *all* the possibilities."

Breath catching, I stared up at him for a long moment, wishing it was light out, that I could allow myself to fall into the depths of his eyes and see everything.

But I couldn't.

Instead, I had to trust in his tone, in the gentle way he held me against him, in his racing pulse and unsteady breaths that matched mine.

And I found I *did* trust in all those things.

But perhaps the thing I trusted in the most was . . . possibility.

It was there. We only had to reach out and grab for it.

"Steady?" he asked what might have been seconds or minutes or *hours* later.

I nodded and he released me, bending to scoop up my heels that had fallen again. At this rate, they would be all scratched up, embedded with sand in the seams and buckles and probably ruined by the time we made it back to the car. But though they'd cost me an exorbitant amount of money, I couldn't summon up the outrage to care.

Shoes. Aaron. Possibility.

It was no competition.

Possibility won hands down every time.

THIRTEEN

Aaron

THE TEXT CAME as I pulled through the gate leading into the winery in Temecula.

I ignored the *buzz-buzz* as I navigated the sedan through the winding driveway. This late in the evening the path darkened and the likelihood of seeing a critter was high. Luckily, I safely avoided any animal interactions and pulled into the one-car garage next to the studio I stayed at while in town.

Smaller than the bunkhouse, but with more modern amenities, the guest suite had become my alternate home base. Carlos and I had similar apartments on every winery we owned, Utah aside. It was something that was ultimately cheaper than us having to rent a house or pay for a hotel room or even rent a car (since we shared the vehicles kept onsite), every time we were in town overseeing the business. Utah was the sole difference because I stayed at the ranch and had never built out the former storage shed Carlos had given me when I'd begun working with him into something livable. He had a nice apartment on-site, and after the last conversation with Warren, however, I would be staying there until I had my own place situated.

I turned off the car, grabbed my wallet from the cupholder, snagged my keys, and let myself into the studio. Only then did I pull my phone from my pocket and glance at its screen.

A breath I hadn't realized I'd been holding slipped free.

Mags.

I'd been trying to pretend I didn't care if it wasn't her. But that was a lie obviously, and seeing her name on the screen, seeing her message made my heart squeeze.

This was the right thing.

We were doing the right thing in grabbing on to the possibility of a future between us.

I leaned my back against the door as I opened the text, feet incapable of moving until I'd read the words this woman had sent me, heart racing, palms a little sweaty. It was almost like I was a teenager again, the anticipation was so great.

Turns out, I'm a fan of wine nerds. Dinner at my house tomorrow?

My mouth actually ached from the giant ass grin that broke out on my face. Then I realized I needed to reply, that I wanted to reply with something equally quippy, something that would make *her* smile.

And I didn't know what to say.

And I'm a fan of tacos, can I eat yours?

Fucking hell. What was I saying about teenagers a moment ago?

I'm a fan of short skirts, can I put my hands under yours again?

Not teenager, but definitely creepy.

When you kiss me, I feel like I can breathe again.

Less creepy. Maybe. But definitely too much after one dinner and a walk on the beach together.

"Shit," I muttered, dropping my wallet in the bowl that sat atop the table I kept in the hallway as a staging post for all the crap that ended up in my pockets at the end of the day.

Today, since I'd emptied them before I'd left to see Mags, in the bowl there were several soil samples Carlos had demanded I collect, his way of ensuring the employee we paid for that was doing his job. I'd label and leave them in his suite before heading out, so he could do his independent testing. Along with the containers of dirt were several receipts I needed to save for reimbursement, a few press requests from the marketing team, a lighter, and a peach-scented candle.

The same candle I'd bought for Mags ten years before, planning on surprising her with it, knowing it was a small thing, but also that it would bring a smile to her face. I'd kept it, put it in my suitcase wherever I went out in the world.

Fuck. I'd known even before I'd *known*.

I tugged off the metal lid, dull from the years that had passed, and ran my fingers along the rounded edge of the glass circle, considering. The wicks were nearly burned to the bottom, even though I'd only lit it judiciously over the years. But I didn't need the past anymore. I had the future. I reached for the lighter, lit the three wicks, and let the soft, sweet scent begin to fill the room.

And then I knew what to say.

Well, lucky this wine nerd has access to plenty of wine. How many bottles should I bring?

My phone vibrated with a response almost immediately.

How about one of those huge wooden casks?

I chuckled.

Not sure that would fit in my car.

*Hmm. *thinking GIF* Two?*

I was still chuckling.

I'll bring three.

My hero.

I laughed outright at that, fingers flying across my cell's screen.

Chardonnay, okay?

Perfect. See you tomorrow around six?

Yes. Mags?

Yeah.

Thanks for—

I stopped typing, backspaced like a mofo, and thought about

the best way to put what was in my head into words on a text screen.

I'm not letting you go this time.

Hitting send before I could reconsider, I spent the next several minutes as I waited for her to respond alternating between relief that I'd gotten it out there and horror that I'd pushed too far, too fast, too soon.

When a good five minutes passed, I sighed and dropped my phone onto the table, breathing in the aroma of the candle, getting lost in the scent.

Yeah.

Too soon. Too fast. Too far.

Damn.

I crossed to the fridge, tugged open the door, and pulled out a beer. Contrary to Mags' teasing, I didn't mind alcohol, though —and I wasn't brave enough to say this anywhere in the vicinity of Carlos—I preferred a cold beer at the end of the day rather than wine.

Popping the top as I walked back to the living-slash-bedroom space, really just a couch and bed positioned near each other in the large open room, I stifled a sigh and sat down on the loveseat.

I was bound to misstep, especially after coming to the realization of how much I wanted her. Certain to err after realizing what a mistake I'd made in holding on to that fury, in letting her go in the first place, in not realizing how strong the connection tying us together was. Tonight, I'd discovered it was still as strong now as it had been a decade ago.

And I knew it was precious.

I could still feel the burn of my hope bursting into flames, reduced to cinder and ash upon seeing her with Talbot and thinking whatever slim chance I had of making things right, of grasping on to the link between us and moving forward, was gone.

But even through that despair, I'd still known what I wanted, had some time to get used to the idea over the last month.

Maggie hadn't.

I'd been angry. Now, inexplicably I wasn't.

Yes, I'd explained my thinking, what had changed, but that didn't magically make things right, even if she did throw me a bone by going to dinner, even if she didn't push me away when I kissed her, even if—

My phone buzzed, and I shot up from the couch so fast that I nearly dumped my beer everywhere.

I fumbled, caught it before more than a few drops escaped, then hurried over to grab my cell from the table, heart tripping, fingers fumbling to unlock the screen. Thankfully, the message was short and easy to read.

Though it didn't calm my heart.

That still raced like a freight train, even as relief poured down my back.

Because her message only said,

Prove it.

I'd typed a reply and sent it back before my brain processed the movement.

I intend to.

We were sitting on the edge of the pool, my jeans rolled up, our feet in the pool, and enjoying the warm evening air.

It was cooler tonight, the warm system that had kept night-time temperatures higher than normal beginning to break down. There was even a threat of rain on the horizon.

I put down my wine glass—see? Even I indulged in the business every once in a while—and lay back, folding my hands behind my head.

"I'm so proud of you for following your dream," I said.

An inhaled breath.

Then the *clink* of her glass—although I guessed glass was actually a misnomer because we'd switched to plastic cups when we'd come over to the pool.

I listened to the rustle of her clothes as she reclined beside me, able to picture the outfit with crystal clarity, even though my gaze was on the night sky. Shorts that had given me plenty of glimpses of those tantalizing thighs, a simple burgundy blouse that highlighted the flecks of gray in her brown eyes, the shining silver bracelet with its peach dangling from the band.

"I am, too," she said, and I shifted to my side, unable to not look at her. "I'm good at my job. I work long hours and it can be thankless sometimes, but I have the best clients, and I've gotten to travel the world, see so many things I never could have imagined."

I ran my fingers down her arm. "Where has been your favorite place to visit?"

Her face lit up, and she rolled over, pulling her feet from the water. "That's an unfair question! I've been too many cool places."

"Nice try," I teased, leaning in to press a kiss to the tip of her nose. "But muahahah! You must choose one!" I added, affecting my evil genius voice, which admittedly sounded ridiculous, even to myself, but because it made her smile, I knew I would keep doing it.

"Goof," she said, sliding closer and flicking her tongue out to caress my bottom lip. "Come on." She pushed up, snagged her wine, and then took my hand, leading me off the pool deck and toward a set of hedges.

"Um," I began when it seemed as though she was going to beeline us right into them.

"Shush." A slight shift of our bodies and I saw that the row of hedges had a small break in them, leading to an enclosed . . . paradise. I couldn't think of any other way to describe it. The walls of greenery completely boxed in the space from the ground to several feet over my six feet. A large tree planted in the center had grown tall enough to cover the square with a canopy made of branches and leaves, strands of lights woven between them. As I marveled at the walls and roof made from nature, I missed what was on the ground. Soft grass, a large blanket and pillows, electric candles interspersed and giving off small, intimate glows.

"This is . . ."

"I know," she murmured, tugging me forward, leading me to the blanket. "Artie and Pierce aren't much for nature, so they let me play with this space when they had the hot tub removed a few years ago. "I added the lights, picked up some outdoor blankets and pillows, candles, flowers."

My gaze followed her when she pointed to something else I'd missed, boxes of bright flowers lining the walls. "Luckily enough, the sun sneaks through in the mornings to allow them to grow. I modeled it after this tiny church in France that Artie's company filmed at a few years ago." She glanced up at me. "I was still just an assistant then, in charge of managing her schedule, making sure she had what she needed so she could focus on the production." Her voice dropped. "I stumbled into an older section and fell in love. Those walls were made of stone, covered in ivy, but I wanted to have the same feeling of being completely wrapped in nature, in quiet, as I felt there."

"It's beautiful," I murmured, slipping my hand free from hers so I could slide an arm around her, tug her close.

She smiled up at me. "In the end, they didn't even end up using that corner for filming, but I'd seen enough to fall in love with it anyway."

"And is this your way of telling me that France was your favorite?" I asked, letting her lead me over to the blanket, taking her glass from her fingers when she lay down so I could lie next to her, so I could gather her against me and hold her tightly.

"One of them."

I nuzzled her neck. "That's cheating."

"I also love Scotland and Australia. New Zealand holds a special place, as does Mykonos, and Iceland, and—"

I laughed, cutting off her words with a kiss. "Tell me, is there any place you *don't* love?"

Mags froze, head tilting to the side as she considered. "I wasn't a huge fan of Costa Rica."

That surprised me.

"I know," she said with a laugh. "It was beautiful, without a doubt, but it was humid and the bugs . . . Hey!" She smacked my chest lightly when I snorted. "You weren't there, mister. They were big and hairy and—"

I kissed her.

Long and slow, with plenty of tongue and plenty of wandering hands.

When we broke away, chests heaving, I rested my forehead to hers, "No bugs." Another press of my lips to hers. "Got it."

"I—" She shook her head. "You're not going to let me live this down, are you?"

I grinned. "I'll protect you from the bugs, I promise."

"You're terrible."

"No," I murmured. "I'm the man who wants to kiss you all over."

"A-aaron."

"It's true."

"I know it's true." She wiggled closer. "Because I want to kiss you all over, too."

I brushed her hair back from her face, rubbed my nose against hers. "I'm glad." A beat. "But we're not going to, Peaches."

She froze, leaned back. "We're not?"

"No," I murmured. "We're going slow and steady. Taking our time to get to know each other again."

"For how long?"

My response was delayed as I considered that, trying to reconcile what I felt for Mags with what I'd had with the other women I'd dated. There had been the rare one-night stand, but that wasn't something I did when I wanted to build a future with a woman. It was more . . . the mutual scratching of itches. "Four more dates."

Cocking her head to the side, she asked, "Why four?"

"It gives you time," I said, "and it shows you this is something more than sex."

"That's stupid."

I blinked. "*What?*" I was trying to be respectful, to give her a chance to come to terms with us, with the future of us, without muddying the waters with sex.

"That's stupid," she said again. "I want you. You want me. We're two consenting adults. We'll use protection and common sense, not some arbitrary number of dates to tell us when it's acceptable to have sex."

Put it that way, and I did feel a bit foolish pinning a number on future intimacy, but . . .

She shifted, pushing me to my back, straddling my waist then leaning forward to cup my cheeks. "I'm not trying to make fun of you, baby." Mags bent so her lips were very close to mine. "I just— I'm attracted to you. I've liked spending time with you, exploring this, and I want to do more of it. Am I ready to jump your bones here and now?" A shake of her head. "Unfortunately, no. Though I'd be down for some heavy petting and groping through our clothes." She bit the corner of her mouth, mischief dancing in her eyes, and that paired with her words had my cock hard and pressing against the zipper on my jeans. The mischief dimmed, the soft fingers of one hand tracing along my jaw. "But do I want to tie us down to a particular date before we can sleep together? No, I don't."

"I want you to be comfortable."

"And *I* want *you* to be comfortable," she said, lying across my chest, arms slipping under my shoulders to hug me close. "But I also don't necessarily want to use Aaron Logic to get there," she added lightly.

"What's Aaron Logic?"

"Maybe Spreadsheet Logic is more accurate."

I snorted, too busy enjoying the feel of her sprawled over me to be offended by her poking fun at me. "Spreadsheet Logic can be a good thing," I said, my arms going around her, sliding up and down the lush curves of her. "It sets expectations, makes our responsibilities clear, allows for routine."

Silence.

Then tinkling laughter.

"What?" I asked, hands pausing, albeit more focused on what was beneath my palms than what I'd been saying.

She stopped, burrowed into the spot where my throat met my shoulder and spoke, hot words against my skin that raised goose bumps on my arms, sent sparks down my spine. "Think about what you just said and repeat it back to yourself—expectations, responsibilities, routine." A flick of her tongue. "Not one of those things is me, Aar."

"Are you saying I need to use less Spreadsheet Logic and more Maggie Peaches Allen Logic?"

"Yes." Her tone was unyielding.

I started laughing.

She joined in, but after a few seconds her laughter trailed off, and she pressed a kiss to my throat. "But I also understand that Spreadsheet Logic is you, Aar. So, I promise you that I'll get better at using it."

"I don't think I've ever heard sexier words come out of your mouth."

She giggled. "Noted." A pause, then she pushed up enough to meet my eyes. "So, in that vein, I'll just say that tomorrow you're taking me on date three—note: I'm giving you the number, so we have Spreadsheet Logic covered—and after which anything beyond heavy petting and copious amounts of groping is on the table—*my* logic."

"Maggie and Spreadsheet Logic combined." I slid my hand a little lower, the curve of her ass just at my fingertips. "I like it."

"Maggie and *Aaron* Logic," she corrected.

My hand slid a little lower. "I like the sound of *that* better."

A grin before she lowered herself again, her next words against my skin. "One ring to rule them all, and all the other nerdy things?"

"Hmm." I was too focused on the curve of her ass so close to my palms, the scent of her in my nose, the feel of her against me.

"Aaron?"

"Hmm?" I repeated.

"Is this your way of telling me you're ready for the wandering hands and heavy petting portion of the evening?"

My cock twitched.

She felt it, hips pressing forward against my erection,

making stars flash behind my eyes, need pulse through every cell in my body.

Maybe I should have used Spreadsheet Logic, slowed us down.

But I didn't want to.

Instead, bringing one hand firmly over her ass, cupping the curves, tugging her more firmly against me, I simply said, "Yes."

Then I kissed her.

And *then* I let my hands wander.

FOURTEEN

Maggie

HE'D SURPRISED ME.

I'd made the long drive from West Hollywood to Temecula this time, though I'd had less of a battle with traffic, seeing as this was the weekend. After spending the morning catching up on emails, arranging some press tours and fine-tuning a lingerie brand Eden was developing, whose business model was to donate a set of undergarments to women in need with every item sold, I'd loaded up my podcast about home winemaking—I figured I had some knowledge to catch up on—and had headed out for the winery.

Now it was midafternoon, and I'd expected the restaurant and tasting rooms to be full of people eating and drinking, enjoying Lakeland Lucha's wares.

And in fairness to all the wonderful things the winery had to offer, they might be.

But about ten minutes from reaching Aaron's business, he'd called and given me directions to a different entrance, a winding road that led to a small cottage-looking building surrounded by grapevines.

Upon closer inspection, it was actually two small cottages joined by a single car garage in the middle. They were cute, Mediterranean inspired with orange stucco walls and red tile roofs, the windows rounded and trimmed with iron accents.

But that was all my mind had time to process.

Because Aaron was on the porch. From the way my heart accelerated, heat arrowing down between my thighs, one would have thought he was naked and glistening like a Greek god, or dressed to the nines in a tuxedo only Pierce could pull off, or maybe Chris Hemsworth in a loincloth—

Maybe *that* should have given me a sign I was in deep, that this was too much, too soon, especially given the whole thinking a loincloth was a good thing. Instead, I was arrested by the sight of Aaron on the porch.

Everything inside me froze for one long moment and then refocused.

Right.

This was what I'd been searching for over the years.

All the living, all the experiences, everything that had been perfect except for that tiniest little niggle . . . *all* of it circled back to Aaron.

I felt a wave of sadness rush over me, wondering if perhaps I'd been wrong all those years ago, thinking we would have never worked out. Maybe we could have beaten the odds, maybe we'd missed out on a full decade when—

My car door opened, even though I didn't consciously remember parking.

"I—"

"Hush," Aaron ordered, reaching over me and turning off the ignition, tugging the keys out and pocketing them.

My eyes stung, my throat burned, my stomach churned because driving up and seeing him waiting for me highlighted exactly how much I'd missed out on. A tear escaped, sliding down my cheek in a scalding trail of moisture, but when I went to wipe it away, he beat me to it, his thumb capturing it before he unbuckled my seat belt and tugged me out of the car.

"B-baby," I said and sniffed. "I—"

Solid arms banded around me, plastered me against his chest. "Hush now," he murmured. "I'm here. It's going to be okay."

The reassurance made another tear fall, another, until they were coming in earnest, until I was sobbing against Aaron's chest. I'd been strong over the years, pretending to be resolute in my decision, using Aaron's mom telling me to go and not come back—in an encouraging, leave-the-nest way, not in a mean one —as proof I'd been right. I'd even convinced myself that Aaron had been the one who'd made the mistake in letting me go, and that it didn't matter anyway because we'd been too young and, in the end, it wouldn't have worked out between us.

But standing there, my body pressed to his, I couldn't help but wonder, what if?

What if we'd made it? What if he'd come? What if I had stayed or gone back or—?

So many questions I would never have the answers to. So many answers I was desperate to know. So many unknowns that sliced at my core and made me doubt everything we'd been through.

And I cried.

For those what-ifs. For the lost past. For not realizing how precious this thing between us was.

Eventually, what felt like an eternity later, I managed to pull myself together. I lifted my head from Aaron's chest, found he'd somehow carried me into the house, had settled us on a couch.

"I'm sorry," I said, voice hoarse. "Some fun date three, huh?"

He cupped my cheek, stared deeply into my eyes. "I'm guessing this wasn't because you had a bad day at work, or somebody honked at you on the freeway."

My eyes slid to the side, and I shook my head. "No."

"Then what, Peaches?"

Eyes back to his, knowing I needed to see him when I admitted, "Driving up and seeing you made me realize exactly what we missed out on."

He sucked in a pained breath.

Tears threatened again.

He saw, the man who'd known I was upset from twenty feet away through a windshield, *of course* he saw the tears coming. Wrapping his arms around me again, he said, "Shh, honey. This is all that matters now. As much as it sucks, we can't go back and change things."

"I broke us," I said. "I just took a hammer to our relationship and shattered us to pieces."

He pulled back, captured my chin between thumb and forefinger and said firmly, "We *both* had our hands on the handle."

"I—"

A slight jostle. "I'm not trying to be a dick here, but what is this accomplishing, Mags? We both have regrets that we can't do anything to change. How is beating yourself up benefiting either of us?" He released my chin, slid his fingers along my jaw to weave into my hair. "It pains me to see you upset, and you've cried yourself hoarse."

I sighed.

Aaron brushed a kiss over my forehead. "We can't go back, Peaches. We have to keep moving forward."

I dropped my head to his shoulder, sighed again. "So, what you're saying is we need to use Maggie Logic."

Laughter that slid over my skin like a warm blanket.

"Yeah, Peaches. We need more Maggie Logic."

I nodded, cuddled closer. "I'm sorry I freaked out."

"Don't apologize for showing me what's in your mind and heart," he said, and his tone was almost harsh. "The future I want to build with you, the one I hope you want to build with me, is about honesty, about truth, about you and me and *never* any secrets. I want you to feel safe to tell me anything. I want you to trust that I will never willingly hurt you."

I'd be lying if I'd said I hadn't waited my whole life to hear those words. But I was too touched to say that, to do more than stammer out, "A-aaron," my eyes stinging again.

He lightly stroked my nape, murmured, "Cry if you need to."

That had the opposite effect of what he probably assumed it would, because it made my tears dry, made laughter bubble in my throat. "I think I'm done." I grinned at him. "For the moment."

His sigh of relief had me laughing again.

But neither of us moved, and we just held each other for long minutes. For my part, I was thinking of how good it was with him, to be held by him in this moment, and I assumed he was feeling the same, especially since his next words were, "So lucky, Peaches."

"Yes," I murmured. "We both are."

His arms tightened, his lips brushed my hair, and the sun moved lower in the windows.

Eventually, it got dark enough to necessitate turning on a few lights, and I remembered the present I'd brought him that was sitting on the passenger seat of my car.

"My loaves!" I cried, in the middle of chopping an onion Aaron had directed me to dice. Apparently, he was cooking his secret pasta sauce recipe for me, and I was to play sous chef. Which, frankly, was fine with me. Baking, I enjoyed. Coming up with meal ideas that didn't involve copious amounts of flour, sugar, and butter were less exciting.

"What?" he asked, turning from the pan where he was frying up some ground beef.

"My loaves!" I said again.

I set my knife down and rushed for the door, hoping it hadn't been warm enough to melt the icing I'd topped them with. It had taken ages to get the right consistency.

"Where are my keys?" I called.

"On the table by the door," he called back.

Nodding, though he probably couldn't see me since he'd turned back to the pan, I hightailed it for the table, searching the cluttered top for a few seconds before locating and scooping up my keys. I'd just started moving again, anxious to rescue those loaves, when I noticed the candle and skidded to a stop.

Sweet Peach.

Fumbling fingers tugged the lid off, saw it had nearly been burned to the bottom. I noticed the peeling label, the slightly dusty ring on the table when I shifted it to the side.

Not something newly purchased. Something that had been around long enough to make a ring, to be burned nearly to the end of the wicks, to—

"Find them—?"

Aaron rounded the corner of the kitchen cabinets, words faltering when he saw me staring at the candle like a lunatic.

"Are you okay?" he asked carefully.

I put the lid down, nodded. Then because I *had* to know, inquired, "What's this?"

His eyes never left mine. "You know how long I've had that candle?" he asked, carefully putting the lid back on.

"No," I whispered.

"I bought it for your birthday."

My breath shuddered out. "But I was already gone." I'd hit the road as soon as school had gotten out for our senior year, not caring that my eighteenth birthday was a week later.

"I know. I almost threw it out when you left, but . . . something stopped me."

Probably the same *something* that stopped me from throwing the peach bracelet out the car window and never looking back. "Aaron," I whispered.

His hand covered mine, lifting it to his chest, where I could feel his heart beating steady and sure beneath my palm. "I've brought that with me everywhere over the years. I've kept that little piece of you with me on my journeys. Careful to only burn it for a few minutes at a time because I knew, just *knew* that when it was gone, I wouldn't be able to get it back." His eyes lifted to mine. "Get *you* back."

I inhaled, released the breath slowly, my body melting against his. "But I'm here now."

"Yes." His expression went soft. "Yes, Peaches, you are." He cupped my cheek. "I love you. I always have, and I'll never stop."

Heart rolling over in my chest, its underbelly exposed, the organ belonging solely to this man, I covered his palm with mine and told him the truth that had been in my mind and soul for almost my entire life. "I love you, too."

His eyes flared hot, fingers spasming against mine.

And I don't know if he bent and kissed me or if I rose on tiptoe to press my lips to his, but all I knew was that I was suddenly in his arms and he was kissing me like he was starving.

And so was I.

Ten years led to this moment.

One hand ran down my spine, clamping over my butt, angling my hips against the hard jut of his erection. I gasped, moved closer, wanting there to be nothing between us, wanting him over me, pressing into me.

His tore his mouth away, fingers digging into my ass, a little rough, but not painful, and his other hand woven between the strands of my hair, hot against my scalp. Rapid, damp exhalations coated my lips. "Peaches?" he asked, hips thrusting forward.

"Yeah?"

"Is this time for Maggie Logic? Or Spreadsheet Logic?" He thrust a thigh between mine, rolled his hips, making me gasp. His cock like granite where it pressed against my stomach, the fingers on my ass encouraging me to ride the long, hard thigh.

Stars were sparking to life behind my eyes, but I managed to get out. "Maggie Logic. Definitely Maggie Logic."

"Thank fucking God," he said, sweeping me up into his arms and carrying me to the bed.

He dropped me to the mattress, but I didn't so much as bounce, he was on top of me that quickly. Bracing himself with one hand by my head, his lips found mine, tongue sliding home, other hand slipping beneath the hem of my T-shirt.

"So. Fucking. Soft," he groaned.

My breath caught when his fingers moved higher, teasing the undersides of my breasts through the satin of my bra, a shiver coursing through me when my nipples beaded against the material.

I reached for his T-shirt. "Off," I ordered.

He sat up, tore it over his head, and I'd tried to take advantage of him moving away to remove my own shirt.

But I wasn't fast enough.

All that quickly, he was back on top of me, only now I had the gloriousness of his naked chest against my bra-covered one, the silky material of my blouse bunched over my shoulders.

He chuckled, a low, masculine sound that had moisture spreading between my thighs. "Trapped, Peaches. Just like I like you." He trailed a finger through the valley of my breasts, sending shockwaves of heat in every direction, my nipples beading and aching for his touch.

A shuddering breath. "A little help?"

"Hmm," he murmured, dipping his head, taking a nipping bite at my side, just beneath my rib cage. "What if I said I like you like this?" I bucked when those teeth closed over my nipple through the fabric of my bra. "Helpless and subject to my every whim."

I groaned when he slid the material aside, sucked my nipple deep, sending wave after wave of pleasure through my nerve endings. "I'd say," I managed to get out as he slowly kissed his way over to my other breast, "that I don't mind being trapped and subject to your every whim." He froze, and I sucked in another breath, got another sentence out. "Especially when the result is your mouth on my breasts."

His breath hissed out between his teeth.

I hitched a leg around his waist, arched up. "I'd just prefer your cock inside me while you're doing it."

"Fuck, Peaches," he said gruffly, the rough words skating down my skin, making my pelvis tilt, and I shamelessly rubbed myself against him. "You're killing me."

I twisted my arms, trying to free them. "I'll kill you some more if you help a girl out."

Silence.

Then movement. The shirt that had been stuck over my shoulders, obscuring most of my vision, pressing down on my nose and mouth, was gone.

Only, it didn't go far.

Aaron tugged it over my head and used it to keep my hands trapped above me, twisting the material to keep my arms in place. "Your breasts," he said, sliding down and rubbing his face against the body part in question, "are the most gorgeous things I've ever seen."

"You've seen them be—"

I broke off when he slid the cups of my bra up. I gasped when he took one nipple in his mouth, when he rolled the other between thumb and forefinger. I moaned when he spent long minutes sucking and petting, driving my desire higher, making me arch and buck against him, desperate for more, for him to be inside me.

Then he kissed his way down, dragging his hot tongue along my skin, flicking open the button of my jeans and yanking them off my legs.

I thought he'd leave my panties in place, tease me through them.

But a moment later, they were gone, slid down my thighs, tossed aside carelessly. He didn't give me a moment to catch my breath, to wonder if I'd taste okay. His mouth pressed to my pussy and he licked me up with a long, slow stroke of his tongue.

I screeched, bucked hard, but thankfully Aaron just held my hips in place and kept his mouth and tongue moving. He remembered all the secret spots we'd discovered together during all those firsts we'd shared, during all of the warm summer nights when we'd snuck into the orchards or into the back of his car or even in one or the other of our bedrooms. The memories were as heady as his tongue, his fingers, and I wound tighter, flew higher, hips moving against his mouth, hands wrapped tight in my shirt, breaths coming in such short gasps I didn't think I'd ever draw in enough oxygen.

And then I froze, perched on the cliff for one long, taut moment.

He pressed his tongue hard against my clit.

I shattered, plummeting over the edge, catapulting toward Earth as wave after wave of hot, delicious pleasure coursed through my body.

Limp, eyes bleary, it took me several minutes to just catch my breath. But as I did, I slowly became aware of Aaron next to me, holding me close, running his fingers along my side as he gently coaxed me back to the present.

"I think I like Maggie Logic," he murmured, bending to kiss me gently.

"Me, too," I said, lips curving as I went to lift my arms, wanting to stroke his face, to hold him close. But the shirt was still tangled, and when I went to free myself, he caught me, held me in place.

"I thought you didn't mind being at my whim."

I wrapped a thigh around his waist. "Only if you promise to give me more Maggie Logic."

He grinned then kissed me until my lungs screamed for air. "I can do more Maggie Logic." Fingers between my thighs, sliding through the dampness, slipping inside. His finger brushed my clit, and I jumped. "Too sensitive?"

I nodded.

He kept the movements light and steady, coaxing me back up, my skin hot and tight, my pussy wetter than it had ever been. This time when he touched my clit, I groaned, pressed up into the touch and said, "I hope to God you have a condom."

"Shh," he said. "For now, just let me touch you." He teased me for a few seconds longer, until my eyelids were heavy, until a sheen of sweat had broken out on my skin, and my hips were undulating against his thumb, his palm. I needed release, but I needed him inside me more.

"Aaron," I cried out, arching roughly, head tossing from side to side on the pillow. "Tell me. You have. A *fucking* condom."

Oak-colored eyes on mine, the flames of desire within them easy to discern.

"Please," I said. "I need you."

A nuzzling kiss to my throat, my jaw, my ear. "Okay, Peaches," he said and reached into the nightstand, extracted a plastic-wrapped square.

"Thank God," I breathed.

He chuckled and the raspy, masculine sound nearly sent me over the edge. But then the condom was on, and he was between my thighs. "Okay?"

"Now," I countered, using my legs to pull him down. The shirt fabric had slipped up to my wrists, and was more hindrance than restraint at that point, allowing me to clutch at his shoulders as he slid home.

"Fuck," I moaned, the hot brand of him stretching, filling me with more than just desire. It filled me with peace, with home, with love. This man was it for me. He'd *always* been it, from the first time he'd kissed me beneath the peach trees back in Utah. We'd gone our separate ways, done our damnedest to shatter the ties between us, but while the bond could be buried or muted or ignored, it couldn't be broken.

This was him. This was me.

This was *us*.

His lips found mine as we moved together, winding higher and higher, need skyrocketing, desire just mere moments away.

"I love you, Peaches," he whispered against my lips.

And I exploded, crying out, convulsing around him, his thrusts gaining in intensity and speed, drawing out my orgasm, aftershocks of pleasure sparking to life throughout my body until I froze, groaning as he planted himself deep, and his release carried him over the edge.

It took a long time to catch my breath, to come back to my body, but when I did, Aaron was propped over me, eyes warm as he watched me. "Hi," I murmured.

"Hi," he said back, brushing the backs of his knuckles over my cheek. "You okay?"

"I'm great."

"Good." He leaned back, tugged my shirt the rest of the way off my arms.

"Wh—"

He came close again, eyes gone hot, burning. "Again," he murmured then pulled me close and slanted his lips over mine. His kiss was everything, incinerating me, somehow filling me with need even though I'd just come twice. I shouldn't be ready to go again, after Aaron had just so effectively taken me over the edge, but I found that as he kissed me, I was right there with him, my desire ramping back up, my need filling my every pore.

Ten years to make up for, I supposed, lacing my arms around his neck and kissing him with everything I had.

His fingers slid south, teasing, making me cry out for wanting him.

Then those fingers went east again, into the nightstand, extracting another condom.

We came together on a pair of matching groans, and I reveled in the rightness, in the way our bodies remembered each other, were able to wring every bit of pleasure from within.

Thus, it wasn't until *much* later that I made it outside to my car to retrieve my loaves. The icing wasn't melted, had actually stayed perfectly in place.

Which was a good thing, because Aaron's secret pasta recipe wasn't in great shape—the pasta had boiled to mush and the sauce was burned, a thick black ring in the pan that told me it would be way too much effort to try and scrub it off.

We tossed the pot in the trash, along with dumping the pasta mush, and took the loaves to Aaron's bed, cuddling close as we broke off and fed each other pieces of cinnamon apple bread.

In the process, the icing warmed and got sticky, coating our fingers.

We got crumbs everywhere.

But that was okay, because more than half the fun was licking them up.

A WEEK LATER, Aaron, Talbot, and I were lounging around Artie's pool, soaking in the afternoon sunshine as we devoured some delicious deli sandwiches that Aaron had picked up.

He and Talbot had developed an easy rapport within about five minutes of Aaron showing up.

But that wasn't a surprise, I guessed.

The quickest way to Talbot's heart was food, and between the giant sandwiches and three bags of chips, along with the several bottles of wine Aaron had brought—and Tal's heart was stolen.

I was just happy to have some sustenance to replenish the calories I was burning off.

I hadn't had this much sex . . . since I was a teenager.

But we were trying to soak it all in before Aaron left for Italy. He would be gone for several weeks to finalize some details for their European market and transportation chain.

My world traveler.

Grinning, I let my gaze drift to the sky, watching the white puffs of clouds drift by as Tal and Aaron talked wine.

"The 2018 vintage—" Aaron's phone rang. "Sorry," he said, glancing at the screen where it lay faceup on the table. "It's the Utah winery. I've got to get this." He grabbed his cell, swiping a finger across the screen and lifting it to his ear as he stood up from the table.

In a food and wine coma, I let my eyes go back to the sky, but when I heard Aaron's terse, "*What?*" I straightened in my seat, concern washing over me.

His face was tense, his questions snapped out. "When? How much is left? How long? *Fuck*." He thrust his free hand through his hair. "Get Katie calling the nearby wineries, see if we can borrow theirs. Have Cal get a hold of our mechanic and if he's not available, there's a mechanic in Darlington with experience in heavy machinery." A pause. "Yeah, that's him. Okay, good job calling me right away. I'll be on the next plane out and there as soon as I can. Keep in touch."

He hung up, dropped his chin to his chest for one long moment. Then he lifted his eyes to meet mine. "I gotta go, Peaches. I'm sorry."

My heart pulsed, but I pushed out of my chair, hurried over to him. "What happened?"

"It was too cold when we harvested, the grapes were too frozen. The team was struggling to press them for juice." He sighed. "They pushed the machinery too far and broke the whole damned thing."

"Oh shit."

He nodded, eyes furious except for a touch of humor at the edges. "Yeah," he muttered. "A *big* oh shit."

"I'm so sorry."

A shrug. "Things don't go to plan sometimes."

I smiled, said lightly, "That's Maggie Logic."

"I don't think I'll make it back before I head off to Italy," he said, curling his hand around the side of my neck.

Disappointment slid through me.

"I know, Peaches," he murmured, tugging me close. "I'm going to miss you, too. Although . . ." He trailed off when I glanced up at him in question "I was going to ask, albeit in a much more gently and coaxing way . . ."

I frowned. "Ask what?"

". . . preferably after I'd given you several orgasms—"

"Aaron," I said, cutting my eyes toward Talbot and seeing he was riveted to our conversation, unashamedly listening in.

"I'm a statue," he said. "Forget I'm here."

I shook my head, sighed as I turned back to Aaron. "What were you going to ask me, baby?"

"Come to Italy with me," he said, brushing back a strand of hair from my face. "With just a brief stop-off in Utah. You can stay at the winery while I get things sorted, go see Tammy, my mom if you want. I know she wants to see you."

My lungs froze, and I started to shake my head. I couldn't go to Utah. For a multitude of reasons, not the least of which I could admit had to do with my father being there and me keeping my promise to myself to stop being a punching bag. What if I went back and things were still the same? What if I didn't stand up for myself? Then everything I'd been thinking and working on over the last months would mean nothing.

Further that, I couldn't just leave on a moment's notice. I had a business. I had clients and responsibilities. "I can't—"

"Sure, you can."

I jumped, such was the power of Aaron—or perhaps it was the shock-inducing request he'd made—but I'd momentarily forgotten that Talbot was there.

"No, I can't—"

"Artie and Pierce are traveling with Brenna. Eden is on her honeymoon," he said, ticking the sentences off on his fingers as he spoke. "And *I'm* on a break and planning on doing exactly nothing for the next month."

"And Kelsey?" I asked. "Or the fact that you don't have an assistant?"

I regretted the question when I saw the flare of pain dance across his face, but when I opened my mouth to apologize he said, "Kelsey's supposed to have her stuff out by tonight, and even a big-time Hollywood celebrity doesn't need an assistant around to do nothing, does he? I'll take the next few weeks to interview and hire someone."

"What if you need to go out? To pick up food." I was grasping at straws here. "Or toilet paper."

He grinned, slipped his arm around my shoulders, and hugged me against his chest, one that was broad and muscular and probably a real shame that it didn't send sparks of desire fanning through me.

Of course, that would have made our working relationship more difficult.

But Tal was like a brother, if I could have had a brother that rivaled a Greek god, who somehow didn't make me feel one iota of sexual desire.

"This isn't 2020. Toilet paper is readily available in a variety of places." He kissed my temple. "Plus, there's such a thing as delivery." His lips drifted to my ear. "You need to do this. You need to go home and put it all to rest."

"But—"

He pulled back, glared down at me as only he could. "No, buts. No regrets and fears. Just live."

Just. Live.

That was the single thing he could have said to end my protest, which the punk probably knew, given the amount of time and soul-sharing we'd done with each other over the years. He dropped his arm, nudged me back toward Aaron. "I'll be fine." A beat paired with another nudge forward. "I promise." Another pause, this one paired with an award-winning smile. "Plus, you'll have Italy to look forward to afterward. Think of all the pasta and wine and hot Italian men."

Aaron growled.

Literally growled.

And while I was gaping at him, wondering where that had come from, he snagged my wrist and tugged my back against *his* chest, wrapped *his* arms around me. My body responded, heat trailing down my spine, seeping into my breasts, between my thighs.

Talbot turned for the guest house, leaning in just far enough to grab his jacket from the hook on the wall, before closing the door, and heading down the walk.

"You're welcome, lovebirds," he called, whistling as he strode away.

Then he paused, glanced pack, eyes darkening.

But he wasn't looking at me.

His narrow-eyed glare was directed over my head. "Hurt her, and I'll rip off your arms and beat you to death with them."

A kiss blown in my direction, a smile that had made many a female heart skip a beat. However, mine was pulsing for a different reason. Because the man was wonderful, because he was a friend.

Because he was my family.

"Damn, he just Hank-ed me," Aaron murmured.

"What?" I asked.

"His character from the Renegade films," he said. "I've been catching up on all your clients' movies that I haven't seen. The Renegade series is my favorite. Great action, and Tal is a total badass."

"They *are* good," I said, still not quite understanding what he was getting at.

"Well, I just always thought actors are *acting*, you know. That there's nothing real about it."

Ah. Now I got it. "Yeah, I mean a lot of it *is* just acting, but there's always a sliver of their real self somewhere in the role."

"Exactly," he said. "And there's definitely a slice of Hank in Tal."

I chuckled. "His glare is that scary?" I teased, even though I knew the power of that glare, had been on its receiving end—and had given into it—far too many times.

"I think my balls are currently shriveled up into my body."

Laughing and shifting so Aaron released me, I turned and faced him. "We don't want that. I like your balls."

He raised innocent brows. "Do you like them enough to go to Utah with me?"

I snorted, shook my head. "Do I have a choice?"

"You always have a choice, Peaches." His hand slid up and down my back. "I just hope in this case you'll choose me." The corners of his mouth twitched. "And not forget that Italy comes afterward."

God, I loved this man.

The thought slid through me so effortlessly that I didn't panic or startle. Instead, it just settled over my skin, my mind, my soul like a warm and comfortable blanket.

I *loved* this man. Enough to want to go anywhere with him. To support him and see this out and . . . I loved *myself*. Enough that I wanted to close the door on the painful memories of my past, that I wanted to connect with the positive ones. I wanted to keep talking to Tammy, wanted to see his mom.

And I needed to talk to my dad.

But to that last one . . . did I though?

Mentally, I stiffened my spine.

Yes, I did.

"What do you say, Peaches?" Aaron asked. "I don't want to

rush you, but I've got to get tickets on the next flight out. Am I buying one or two?"

Fuck, I loved this man.

Squeezing his hand, I brought my lips to his. "Two, baby."

Then I kissed him, a hot, fleeting caress, before pulling back.

"Where are you going?"

"I need my go-bag," I called, rushing into the house. "And a heavier jacket because Utah is going to be freezing."

His laughter chased me all the way to the bedroom.

FIFTEEN

Aaron

I SLIPPED into Carlos's apartment at the winery, bone-weary after the day.

We'd been able to borrow a press from a nearby winery, but it hadn't arrived until a couple of hours ago on a rented big rig. Before that, Dale, the mechanic I knew from Darlington, the next town over, had managed to cobble the press together enough for it to work at a quarter speed.

Which meant the rest of the crew and I had worked through the night, pressing the grapes the old-fashioned way before they thawed.

Hard, exhausting work.

But we'd salvaged the crop, and the rest of the grapes were currently being processed, the juice collected, the months-long fermentation process beginning.

A process that didn't involve me.

I needed sleep. I needed to hold my woman. I needed sleep.

In that order. Or maybe another, I couldn't be sure, not with my mind so bleary. I rested one hand against the wall, started to toe off my shoes, but nearly stumbled.

That was when I felt warm hands on my back.

"Here, baby," Mags said. "Come with me." She tugged me down the short hall that led to the bedroom, and I nearly collapsed on the edge of the bed.

"I'm filthy," I managed.

"I've got you." Her fingers went to my boots, unlacing and removing them with rapid efficiency, then she tugged my shirt over my head and pulled back the covers on the bed, encouraging me down onto the mattress. Exhaustion swept over me like a black wave the moment my head hit the pillow, but I was alert enough to help lift my hips when she began peeling my sticky jeans from my legs.

"Not how I want you to undress me," I slurred.

"Hush now," she chided and disappeared, footsteps trailing off as she left the room.

I wanted to go after her, to catch her hand and drag her into bed alongside me, but I couldn't summon the strength. And she was back in a few moments, anyway. I didn't open my eyes when she wiped my face free of juice, my hands and arms. "I'll just go put this away," she whispered, "and we can go to sleep—*oh!*"

I'd managed to snag her hand that time, tugging her under the covers next to me.

"I'll put it away later," she said, laughing as she snuggled close.

"Sleep," I grunted.

"Okay, baby."

We didn't talk after that, and I fell headlong into sleep.

I WAS so exhausted that I didn't recognize the persistent pounding for what it was.

"Shit," I distantly heard Mags mutter, moving out from beneath my arm, slipping out of the covers.

"Mmm," I groaned.

"I'll be right back, baby," she murmured, pulling the covers up, pressing a kiss to my forehead. Her footsteps padded over the carpet and disappeared down the hall.

Sleep pulled me back under, so deeply that I didn't hear the voices at first, that I wasn't aware of what was happening on the other side of that wall, that I didn't know what battle Maggie was fighting, or how important it would be to her, to *our* future.

I didn't know.

Didn't wake.

Until it was too late.

For a long time after that morning, I wished I'd recognized the pounding for what it was. I wished I'd known it was a knock, wished I'd known who'd come to the door.

But I *didn't* recognize it.

I didn't hear it.

And because of that, I failed in my promise to protect the woman I loved.

SIXTEEN

Maggie

MY BREATH FROZE in my lungs when I saw the man standing on the porch.

"Where is she?" my dad snapped, shoving me back roughly, making me stagger and catch myself against the doorframe.

"Who?" I asked, rubbing at the aching spot on my shoulder.

"Her! Marleen. She's supposed to be here. She's—" He spun around, lifted his hands like he was going to grab me.

"Don't," I ordered, leaving the door open in case I needed an out.

My father . . . wasn't himself. His eyes were glazed, a crazed look on his face.

"*You.*" He pointed a finger at me. "Marleen."

I watched, shock rippling through me as his expression crumpled, as tears began pouring down his face.

"Why did you leave? Why did you go?"

"I—" His words froze me in place as I tried to process what was happening. Clearly, this was some sort of psychotic break or —my gut sank when I remembered what Claudette had reported to me in our last call. Some forgetfulness, some anger. She'd been worried it was some early signs of dementia and had wanted to get him in to see his doctor.

I'd agreed, of course, but I had silently rolled my eyes. Who wasn't forgetful as they approached their seventies? And my dad had never had any shortage of anger.

"You," he said and moved so fast that he managed to get a hold on the T-shirt I'd worn to bed. He shook me roughly as I tried to loosen his grip. But he was surprisingly strong in this moment, or had super strength, or—

His hand came to my throat.

That was the moment I recognized just how serious of a situation I was in.

His hand clasped tight and I jerked, trying to lurch out of his grip, and for . . . one . . . long . . . moment it didn't seem like I was going to get free. But then I managed to bend back one of his fingers, managed to slip away.

I gasped, coughing and sucking in air, running for the hall. For Aaron.

Hands on my shoulders, weakening, struggling to find purchase. "Why did you leave, Marleen? *Why?*"

"Aaron!" I shouted. "Aaron, I *need* you!"

My father wrapped his arms around my waist, collapsing to the ground, starting to pull me down with him, his eyes furious again.

But Aaron didn't wake, didn't come.

Shit.

"Aaron!" I yelled again, trying to push my dad off, but it was like trying to shift a sack of bricks. "Aaron!"

For several terrifying seconds I heard nothing, but then voice raspy from sleep, "Mags?" reached my ears.

"Help!" I screamed.

Footsteps pounded on the floor as fingernails bit into my

skin, a disjointed chant of "Marleen. Why?" filling the space between us. I knew my dad wasn't in there. For as gruff and mean as he could be, he'd never hurt me physically. This was something else. Like he was lost in some prison in his mind . . . and it had turned him violent.

"Mags?"

Aaron's voice was in the hall now, and I allowed myself to relax slightly. "Here," I said. "Hurry. *Please*."

"Wh—"

My father's weight left me, crashing into the wall at my right before Aaron could finish the question. "What the fuck is going on?" he asked, grabbing my hand, pulling me up and behind him.

"My dad," I said, "h-he's not right."

Aaron rotated to see my father claw himself to his feet, eyes scary and unseeing. "Marleen!"

"Call 9-1-1," Aaron ordered, blocking my father when he reached for me. "Go, Peaches. Hurry."

I nodded, raced to the bedroom for my cell phone, and made the call.

Then, still on the line, I hurried back out, wanting to help, wanting to do something. But there wasn't anything I could do. Aaron was at my dad's side, arm wrapped tightly around his shoulders as my father sobbed into Aaron's knees.

"Marleen. Marleen. *Marleen*."

I heard the name chanted over and over and over again. I heard it as the sirens of the ambulance approached. I heard it in the hospital later that night.

I heard it in my sleep.

I heard it in my dreams for weeks and months to come.

I heard it until I didn't think I could stand to hear it again.

I'D MISSED ITALY.

Or rather, Aaron had put it off until we managed to get the situation with my dad under control.

Dementia.

We'd missed the signs until it was too late.

I stared at the man who'd raised me, the one who'd left so much to be desired, and wondered if he understood what was happening.

The ranch was being sold.

He was being moved into a care facility.

The only positive about the last was that Claudette had applied for and accepted a job there. She was the only person he seemed to recognize anymore, and despite her feeling guilty that he'd managed to sneak out from the house while under her watch, I didn't blame her. She was one person and had to sleep sometime. If either of us had thought it would have gone that bad that fast, we . . . well, we wouldn't have waited until he could get into the doctor's office.

We would have demanded an appointment, intervention. *Something*.

But real life was messy and unpredictable, and I was just happy she'd taken the job and would be spending a couple of mornings a week with my father.

He was definitely the calmest when she was around.

I checked my watch, saw it had been nearly thirty minutes since my dad had been officially discharged. We were currently sitting in his hospital room, waiting for our wheelchair escort out to the parking lot where the care facility would meet us and take him over to get settled.

I hated the thought of doing that too him, but I knew that I didn't have the skills necessary to take care of him.

God, he looked so small sitting in the bed.

But he was strong. Powerful. I still had bruises on my throat and scratches down my back. Even if I quit my job, I couldn't safely take care of him if he had another violent outburst. As guilty as I felt for not recognizing there was a bigger issue at play with his increasingly dark moods, I was also scared.

He'd hurt me.

"I did that."

I blinked, glanced up from my phone. "What?"

"I did *that*." He pointed at me. "I bruised you."

My lungs froze. "It wasn't really you, Dad," I said carefully. He'd been on edge from the moment he'd been admitted, agitated and not fully present—as though something inside him had shifted, had been permanently broken by what had happened a few days before. "I know you didn't mean to."

His chin wobbled and he turned away, eyes on the door. "I hurt you."

"Yes," I said, when it seemed that he was waiting for me to answer.

"But that's not the only place, is it?" His head snapped back, tone sharp and familiar, and I nearly gasped at the first sign of lucidity in days.

"Dad?" I asked.

"I was a bastard," he said. "I'm sorry. I—she left, and you were so much like her—" His chin wobbled again, gaze clouding, that moment of lucid gone in a blink. "Marleen. Marleen left me. *She* left me."

Slowly, I pushed out of the chair and crossed to him. "She did leave," I said gently. "She didn't want to go, though. She wanted to stay."

Wet eyes flashed to mine. "She wanted to stay?"

I nodded. "Yes, Dad."

He released a breath, tears dripping down his face. "She wanted to stay," he repeated quietly.

"Yes."

Marleen was my mom. I missed having a mom every day. I just hadn't realized my dad had missed her, too. He was always so angry if I mentioned her. Furious if I asked questions or if he even heard her name.

I'd just figured he'd cauterized her out of his life, like he'd done me.

But . . . I was starting to see it wasn't that simple.

I sighed, feeling both at peace and cheated out of a resolution. Much of the anger wasn't my fault. Instead, it was wrapped up in the past, in loss, in a mind that was slowly losing itself. But part of me, the portion that couldn't pinpoint when this sickness had begun (my childhood, ten years ago, a month before) was struggling. If it was recent, I wanted to confront my dad with the things he'd done, make him see and understand how wrong he'd been in how he had raised me, how he had treated me. Hell, I'd spent the flight over to Utah two nights ago, planning every word.

Instead, I got *this*.

A cloudy gaze. A mind clawed to pieces by the past.

A father I didn't recognize.

Confronting him in this state would be like kicking a puppy.

No one could tell me exactly when his brain had begun malfunctioning. No one knew if my whole childhood had been molded by the creeping onset of the disease. So no, I couldn't confront him. There would be no pleasure, no relief, no absolution. Just more guilt.

A knock on the door had us both looking up, both watching as it swung open and a nurse pushed a wheelchair in. "Your chariot awaits," she announced chipperly and proceeded to load my father up with efficient speed. "Got everything?"

I nodded, moved to hold the door open.

We rode the elevator down, the nurse the only one talking as she chattered about the snow outside, the storm coming in, the roads, the stars . . . she talked more than I reasonably wanted to hear, but I was almost thankful for the chatter to distract me from the fact that I was trapped in a metal death box, the sides pressing in on me.

Almost because . . . it was a lot of chatter.

It wasn't until we'd met the van for the care center in the garage, gotten my dad loaded up and buckled in, that I realized he'd felt the same about the nurse's babbling.

His fingers snagged my wrist, mischief in his eyes as they met mine. "Blabbermouth," he muttered.

I chuckled, mostly in surprise, then nodded in agreement. "Yes."

He smiled, leaned forward, and his cool lips brushed a kiss on my forehead. "Love you, Maggie girl."

Every muscle in my body went ramrod stiff. I don't think—I couldn't ever remember a time he'd kissed me, when he'd said he loved me. *Ever*. But before I could pull myself out of my stupor, he said one more thing that didn't give me complete resolution, didn't make me forget and forgive everything that happened. Instead, it simply . . . repaired one broken piece inside my heart.

But it was still a precious gift.

Because it was a promise. And I'd had far too few of those in my life from this man.

"Won't hurt you again, baby girl."

The engine turned on as the impact of those words hit home. I stepped back so they could close the doors, watched as the van drove away, tears dripping down my cheeks.

Then I paused, knowing I should head to my car, but unable to make my feet move.

Warm arms around my middle, gentle hands turning my body into his.

"It's okay, Peaches," Aaron whispered into my hair. "It'll all be okay."

"He said he loved me."

Aaron froze.

"He said he was sorry."

Silence, then a slightly rough palm on my cheek. "Did it give you what you needed?"

I shook my head. "No," I admitted. "But I think it gave me some place to start."

He dropped a soft kiss to my lips. "That's something then."

"Yes."

Arms banding tight, he held me to him for a long time, but even with the warmth of his chest, eventually I began shivering. "Come on," he said, "Let's go get pancakes."

"Pancakes?"

It was three in the afternoon.

"They'll help," he said. "I promise."

And he was right.

They did help.

SEVENTEEN

Aaron

I'D EXPECTED a protest when Mags saw me pull in to my parent's house.

Instead, she just walked quiescently beside me up the walkway and into the warmth of the house.

My mom had a bottle of cleaner in her hands, a towel tossed over one shoulder, but when she saw Maggie, she set both down, right in the middle of the floor, and rushed over, hugging Mags tight.

"Oh, babes, I'm so sorry," she said, releasing Mags and shepherding us into the kitchen.

Maggie followed without protesting, didn't say a word when she was nudged into a stool. Nor when I mentioned to my mom that I'd promised her pancakes. She was silent. Quiet. Reduced.

Not. Maggie.

Alarm bells blared to life in my brain.

My mom didn't seem panicked, however. She just nudged me to the fridge and ordered me to start pulling out ingredients. Oranges for fresh juice. Berries to be washed and placed in a bowl. Milk and butter for the pancake batter. I did each task as commanded, but my instincts were screaming.

I didn't like the blank look on Maggie's face.

"Patience," my mom whispered.

And then I got it, then I understood instinctively why I'd brought Maggie here instead of the winery.

Because my mom was giving her something only she could.

I didn't notice it at first. But eventually I did clue in to what she was doing.

Every time my mom moved around the space—to the pantry to grab flour, to a cabinet for glasses for the juice, to the hallway so she could retrieve the bottle of cleaner and the towel she'd left on the floor—she made sure to pass by Mags, to touch her.

A stroke on the arm. Brushing her hair back. A gentle pat on the shoulder.

Grounding her in the here and now.

This wasn't about pancakes. It was about family. About having a parent who could show her what it was like to be part of one, to enfold and hold her tight when things were tough.

This was about my mom giving Mags some Mom Powers.

"Using those powers for good," I whispered, still squeezing oranges and not making much progress to filling up the pitcher as my mom had commanded.

"It'll be okay, honey," she whispered back, brushing a kiss to my temple. "Trust me."

"I don't want her hurting."

"Unfortunately, you can't protect her from all the hurts of the world."

I knew she was right. I still hated it, though.

But instead of moping about it, I kept juicing oranges, continued keeping an eye on the woman I loved, and I learned. I took over on the touches. I took over on grounding Mags here. I brushed a kiss on her cheek. I stroked my fingers through her hair. I whispered I was there if she needed anything. I made sure she knew I was her family and that I wasn't letting her go.

Even with all of that, she was still quiet and withdrawn.

Not catatonic, as she seemed to be tracking everything, but just in shock, retreating from the pain, and scared.

Enough.

I dropped the orange I was juicing, crossed over to her, and pulled her into my arms. "I'm here," I told her, nuzzling at her throat. "I love you." She shuddered. "I'm not leaving and I'm going to keep pushing you until you realize that none of this is your fault, until you realize you're the most incredible woman I've ever known, until you realize I'm not going to stop pestering you until you're *my* Maggie again."

Brown eyes cleared, focused on mine, and she lightly ran her fingers over my jaw. "I would have thought you liked quiet Maggie."

Relief rippled through me at the gentle teasing. "Peaches," I muttered, banding my arms tighter around her. "You scared the shit out of me."

"Sorry," she whispered. "I had a lot to process."

I leaned back, cupped her cheeks in my palms. "Well, next time, process it *with* me."

Her lips twitched. "Is that Maggie Logic?"

"It's Aaron Logic," I growled, dropping my hands and yanking her against my chest again. "I fucking love you."

She sniffed. "I love you, too." A beat. "You can let go now. I'm okay."

"No fucking way."

"Language!" my mom interjected, pulling a pack of bacon from the fridge, a cookie sheet from the drawer, and bringing it over to where Mags had been sitting. "Now time to stop wool-gathering and earn your keep," she snapped, even as her eyes danced.

Mags blinked. "I'm sorry, what?"

"Bacon on the sheet. Sheet in the oven."

Mags studied the items in front of her before her gaze drifted to the oven and she nodded. "Okay."

My mom snapped a towel at me. "More orange juice, peon!"

Mags giggled.

And just like that, she was back.

The numbness had faded, the pain receded enough for her to be here. With me. With us. I knew it wouldn't always be that way, that there was too much pain in her past for everything to be easy and smooth sailing. But I also knew now what to do.

I knew how to be her family.

I knew how to be stubborn.

I knew how to use Maggie Logic to never let her go.

So, using the instincts that logic had honed, I ignored the orange juice. I ignored the bacon.

I held her tighter, and I kissed her with every ounce of love I had.

And *then* I made the orange juice.

EPILOGUE

PART ONE

Maggie, Five months later

I WAS SPRAWLED on my stomach on a blanket, the spring sunshine filtering over my shoulders.

I was supposed to be reading a book, but I'd given up on that a few hours ago in favor of letting the sun's rays warm my back. It was May, so the temperatures were mild and in the low seventies. Perfect weather to sleep away a sunny afternoon while one's boyfriend was working.

Grinning, I nestled into the blanket, letting my eyes stay shut, enjoying the first bit of rest and respite I'd had since December.

Christmas had been spent in Utah with Aaron's family, after having made sure my dad was settled and taken care of in the facility. It had meant working remotely, coordinating with Sam and giving my assistant some herculean tasks.

But the internet hadn't failed me.

And neither had Sam.

After the holiday, we'd flown back to L.A. and traded nights between the winery—where Aaron was overseeing a large construction project—and the guesthouse at Artie and Pierce's.

Then had come awards season.

My busiest time of year, and with complete and utter shit timing, the studio had stacked one of Talbot's releases to come directly after that.

I don't think I saw Aaron awake for more than a couple of hours a week for the last three months.

But I saw him asleep plenty.

No matter what hour I crawled into bed next to him, he never failed to wrap an arm around me and pull me close, to hold me tight, to show me I was important and precious and valuable.

And yes, that was Maggie Logic.

Trust my instincts. Just live.

Yeah, I'd been doing that.

And now, we got to do a little *living* in Italy.

I barely felt the air shift before soft fingers traced the curve of my smile, before I smelled the scent that was solely Aaron, before I felt the man I love lie down next to me and tug me close.

See?

He loved me.

"I thought you were supposed to be reading," he murmured.

"Mmm," I said, stretching against him, not oblivious to the erection poking into my backside. "I decided to nap instead." I rubbed closer, nuzzled against his chest.

He groaned when my hips brushed his. "I like sleepy Peaches."

I snorted. "That sounds like a bad name for a bar."

"Hmm." A chuckle, a nip on my jaw when I rubbed against his cock again. His fingers slipped under the hem of my skirt, pressed against bare skin, dipped between suddenly trembling thighs. "Yes?" he asked, sliding them higher until they reached the damp heat of my pussy.

I bit my lip, glanced around.

"We're alone," he said. "I told Carlos to send everyone home early."

My pulse leaped, and I let my legs fall open. "Did you now?"

"Yes." He kissed me, unfurling heat in my stomach, driving me crazy as he filled me with pleasure, wound my desire tight. A thumb circling and pressing against my clit, warm kisses on my throat, rough fingers pushing the straps of my dress to the side, nipping at my skin and soothing the slight stings with his tongue.

And all the while the sun shone, the wind blew, the smell of the earth and vines surrounded us.

It was peaceful. It was perfect. It—

"Oof!" I gasped when Aaron suddenly covered me with his body.

"What—?"

I'd missed the footsteps.

Because aside from the sun and wind and plants, there were *footsteps*, too. I glanced up to see Carlos, who I'd met all of three times, stumbling away from us with his hands clamped over his eyes. "You said you were going to feel the earth, to talk to the vines with your bare feet, not your bare—"

"Finish that sentence and you're in charge of spreadsheets," Aaron growled.

Carlos kept his eyes covered. "So, you don't need my help to talk to the grapes?"

"No!" we both exclaimed.

"Fine," Carlos said, hands still up as he made his way back down the hill.

I sat up, bit my lip to keep from laughing as I straightened the straps on my dress, smoothed down the skirt.

"I'm sorry," Aaron said, tugging me close and kissing the top of my head.

"Think of the story we'll have to tell."

He froze, mouth dropping open. But his eyes were warm and full to the brim with love. "Yeah, Peaches," he whispered, leaning down so the words puffed against my lips. "Think of the story we'll have to tell."

He kissed me, and I felt the love, felt the ties of family, felt them down to the very marrow of my bones.

But I still had Maggie Logic.

I could still surprise this man.

Which was why I broke the kiss and leaned over to pick up the box that I'd hidden under my book.

I held it out. "I know it's ten years past due, but will you marry me, Aaron Weaver?"

His smile was huge, spreading through his body as he launched himself at me, kissing every inch he could reach. "You drive me crazy, you know that, right?" He nipped my nose. "I had this all planned out. A sunset stroll, romantic words, a giant diamond ring, and you had to go and just hand *me* a ring?"

I grinned. "You know you love it."

He grinned. "Yes, yes, I do."

"For the record," I said, ignoring the way his hand was sliding under my skirt again, "I don't need the stroll, though the words would be nice."

He shifted to nudge one strap of my dress back down then the other. "And the ring?" he murmured against my throat.

"Meh—" I began but broke off with a peel of giggles as he tickled me. "Okay, yes. *Yes!* I want the ring." He stopped and I touched his cheek, making sure he saw the truth of my words.

"But more than any of that, I want you, baby. I want us. I want forever."

"Maggie Logic," he whispered, his eyes shining.

"Maggie *and* Aaron Logic," I countered.

"The best kind."

"Agreed."

He pressed a hard, fast kiss to my lips. "So, about that talking to the vines with our bare—"

"Aaron!"

But then he kissed me again, kissed me so intensely, with so much desire and temptation and need, with so much *love* that suddenly I forgot about Carlos, about being out in the open.

I forgot about everything except Aaron.

Well, everything except Aaron, *and* our naked, bare-skinned communication with the vines.

Funny story, but as time went on, as days turned to years turned to decades, every wine critic always said *that* year's Lakeside Lucha vintage was the best.

I always smiled when I heard that, held the truth close to my heart.

Because I'd found out that, every once in a while, if you talked to the vines, to the earth with bare—

Heh.

Well, anyway, I'd discovered that, every once in a while, the vines could talk back.

EPILOGUE

PART TWO

Talbot

I LISTENED to the sounds of the party on the other side of the hedges, and I knew I should be out there, schmoozing and charming and making sure everyone was happy and having a great time.

This had been my idea, after all.

To surprise Maggie and Aaron with an engagement party after their return from Italy.

I'd helped Aaron pick the ring, plan the words he was going to say.

Then I'd helped Maggie do the same.

A race down the aisle, that Mags had won.

Not that it was a surprise. She was the smartest, most beautiful, most *alive* person I'd ever met.

If only there'd been a spark between us.

But that was the problem.

I didn't feel sparks. I didn't feel much of *anything*. I poured everything I had onto the screen. I worked until every emotion in me was gone . . . and then when they came back, I did it all over again. And again.

And again.

But even giving everything I could, the itchy sensation never went away.

I was FOMOing. I was missing out on something more.

But what?

I'd climbed from obscurity to leading roles. Most even with great scripts . . . or at least feel-good, fun storylines that were a blast to make. I had several houses and cars. I was the face of multiple products, including a delicious Chardonnay.

What could I possibly want or need or be missing out on?

A woman.

Unfortunately, as much as I tried to pretend that wasn't the issue, deep down it was at the crux of everything. I had friends, *good* friends, but it wasn't the same. I wanted what Mags had, what Artie and Pierce had, and what Eden had.

More. *Everything.*

But it was elusive, that everything, especially when I couldn't walk down the street without being photographed, when I couldn't be certain that someone in the business wasn't using me to move up, or worse, would sell me out to the tabloids.

I was one of the most successful men in the world, and I was lonely.

Sighing, I pushed off the tree I'd been leaning against—hiding behind—and knew this wasn't a problem I could fix tonight. I needed to leave my safe little enclave and put myself back out there.

Even though I'd given myself the mental pep talk, I hadn't so much as taken a step toward the exit, when the woman walked in.

Or rather, limped in.

She walked right over to the tree and placed a palm against

it, using her free hand to yank off her heels. "Ow," she muttered, chucking one at the hedges. "Fucking heels." She tore off the other. "Stupid, fucking death traps." The heel sailed through the air, bouncing off the leaves and landing with impressive accuracy near its partner. Then she started lifting the edge of her skirt, muttering about "Stupid pantyhose," and I realized my mistake.

I should have announced my presence before the disrobing began.

I should at least do it *now*.

But I found myself frozen, arrested by the golden skin revealed as she peeled down the stockings inch by inch, the glimpse of black lace when the hem of her skirt slid the wrong—or rather, the *right,* in my opinion—way.

Curves I could hold on to. Softly gilded skin. Ass. Hips. Breasts. Face. They were all incredible, but it was her legs that made my mouth go dry with the need to trace my tongue over. Every. Single. Inch.

In fact, I was so focused on the sight of her legs that I missed her arm moving behind her, missed the fact that one of those shapely thighs had a black holster strapped around it, that her luscious curves hid a gun.

A gun that was now pointed in my direction with rock-steady hands.

"Who the fuck are you?" she snapped.

MEET CUTE

Coming April 5th, 2021
Preorder Talbot and Tammy's story at www.
books2read.com/MeetCute

LOVE, CAMERA, ACTION

Dotted Line

Action Shot

Close Up

End Scene

Meet Cute

LOVE, CAMERA, ACTION

Did you miss any of the other Love, Camera, Action series books? Check out excerpts from the series below or find the full series at http://elisefaber.com/LoveCameraAction

---

Dotted Line

Love, Camera, Action #1

Get your copy at books2read.com/DottedLine

Olivia

THE COLD VOICE hit my spine before I made it to my chair.

"What did you say?"

Cole McTavish.

A tall hunk of a former hockey player, all muscled thighs and towering height, with a face that would have been classified as beautiful if not for the several-times-broken nose, the jagged scar along his jaw, and the small, smooth one bisecting his left eyebrow.

Further that, he was about as opposite from me as anyone I'd ever met.

Relaxed, always ready with an easy smile, Cole never raised his voice—at least *off* the ice. On it, he'd been a terror, a virtually unstoppable force who'd fought when needed and didn't back down from protecting a teammate.

I'd also been his agent while he was playing.

After he'd retired, I'd transitioned him over to Devon, who'd helped him refine his brand for post-playing opportunities. Now, he was the face for a few hockey companies and one well-known corporation that sold watches. Though, to my and the rest of the female populace's dismay, he'd turned down the swimwear ads.

I'd been with him in the locker room enough to know what was under those flannel shirts and jeans.

It was definitely billboard worthy.

Lane started to push by him, but Cole grabbed his shoulder and stepped into my office, forcing Lane back.

Devon Scott trailed them in, a stormy expression on his face.

I glanced at my boss and shook my head, silently telling him I'd already handled it, but Dev shook his head firmly back at me. Which was when I realized that what Lane had said must have been worse than I'd thought. Normally, Devon would never get involved in an argument between my employees and myself unless I asked him to.

Which I didn't.

Since I handled my own shit.

"Tell her what you said."

My gaze flashed to Cole and his darkened face. "It's—"

Emerald eyes locked onto mine, sparking fire. "Tell her," he said, and Lane must have realized exactly how deep of a pile of shit he'd dived into because when I broke Cole's stare to glance at my assistant, his face had gone pale.

I rested my hip against my desk. "I don't need to hear it. Lane, get the file."

Devon crossed his arms. "Tell her," he said. "If you're man enough to mutter it under your breath, you're man enough to say it aloud."

Lane shook off Cole and spun to face me. "Fine," he snapped. "I said that you're such a fucking bitch."

My lips curved and I huffed. "Okay, great, thanks. Now, back to work."

Lane's jaw fell open.

A curl of amusement crept onto Dev's face.

Cole appeared even more infuriated.

Lane somehow went paler. "Wh-what?"

"I've got a ton of work," I told him, "and you say bitch like it's a bad thing." I transferred my gaze to Cole and Dev. "*All* of you are acting like it's the worst insult in the world." I laughed. "Believe me, I've been called worse."

"It's unacceptable," Dev said, and I loved the guy for it.

But this was also the way of the world.

Most men despised strong women. We were told to smile or look happy or be fine with the scraps they tossed our way. If I'd had an issue with men calling me a bitch, I would have quit this male-dominated field ten years ago when I'd been a lowly assistant like Lane and my boss had been a lot worse than a bitch.

But I hadn't.

I'd put my head down, got my shit done.

And I'd learned to not give two craps when a man thought I was a bitch.

Because it had become my anthem.

When I negotiated my client to have equivalent perks in their contract, I was a bitch.

When I demanded a different client have access to the same off-season training as the rest of the team, I was a bitch.

When I secured a bonus that was similar to the rest of the big names on the roster, I was a bitch.

So, fine.

I was a bitch.

Great. Congrats. Moving on.

—Get your copy at www.books2read.com/DottedLine

Action Shot

Love, Camera, Action #2

Get your copy at books2read.com/ActionShot

Artie

"A lady doesn't give away her secrets."

Stormy gray-blue eyes went hot. "I bet I can convince you."

My pussy clenched. Straight up, right then. With a single look. *Uh-oh.* "I don't date children."

He laughed. "I'm twenty-two. That's hardly a child."

"Pierce. I'm thirty-seven."

"So?"

He meant it, too, I could tell.

"So, I don't date people who work with me."

His laughter burned a hole straight down to my middle. "I think we've quite established the fact that we're not going to be working together."

He had a point. And the stink knew it, given the way those hot eyes traced me up and down.

"Eat your pasta," he ordered huskily. Normally orders from men pissed me off, especially men who were many years younger than me, who deigned to think they had a right to give me orders, but there was something about Pierce's gaze, heavy with approval and desire, that made it less annoying and more . . . promising.

I lifted a brow. "And if I don't?"

"I'll just have to—" He broke off and waggled his brows, making like he was going to grab my plate.

I lifted my fork threateningly.

He laughed, went back to his own entrée. "Thanks for lunch."

My carefully constructed bite of pasta fell onto my plate. "I thought we'd established *you* were paying," I said and when he did nothing more but chuckle and then smolder at me again, before continuing to devour his lunch, I knew I was in trouble.

Then deep shit when he snagged the waiter and handed him his card.

And then falling down into a crevice of even deeper shit when he gently tugged my ponytail out from underneath the collar of my jacket when I slipped it on.

Between the table and front door, I considered my options.

At the front door, I made a decision.

I took his hand and pulled him over to my car.

—Get your copy at www.books2read.com/ActionShot

Close Up

Love, Camera, Action #3

www.books2read.com/Closeupef

Eden

Smiling to myself, I reached into my purse for my keys then promptly dropped them to the ground.

Ugh.

I bent—

"I know that ass."

A gasp of outrage on my lips, I straightened and whipped around, ready to tell off the arrogant bastard who'd dared—

Damon Garcia.

Photographer extraordinaire and—

He grinned.

Man who still wanted to get into my pants.

Now, I wasn't a prude. I slept around enough to have been called a whore by more than one publication. It wasn't like my activities between the sheets were more than most men in Hollywood, but because I was a woman, it was noticed and frowned upon.

I just couldn't bring myself to care.

I practiced consensual, safe sex.

If we both were attracted to each other and it was safe, then I didn't hesitate to go for what I wanted.

Maybe that made me a whore.

Maybe I didn't care what other people thought about me.

But Damon?

Damon, I didn't sleep with.

Damon, I didn't fuck or kiss or touch.

Because I knew if I allowed myself a taste, I would never have enough.

I was frozen in place when he bent in front of me and picked up my keys, extending them toward me. That was when I made my first mistake. My fingers brushed his as I took them back. Heat exploded up my arm, my stomach went tingly, and my voice was breathy as I asked, "What are you doing here?"

"I live here now. Well, not the hospital—I'm visiting a friend—but here in town." He smiled, and that paired with the news of him being in L.A. hit me hard upside the head. So hard, it knocked my common sense loose and allowed me to make my second mistake.

Because I didn't run after I'd said, "Oh, that's great."

My third came when he asked, "Want to grab a drink tonight and catch up?"

To which I said, "Yes," instead of "Absolutely not."

My fourth?

Well, my fourth came when I finally gave in to the draw that was Damon Garcia and woke up naked in my bed beside him.

And then he wouldn't leave.

—Get your copy at www.books2read.com/Closeupef

Meet Cute

Love, Camera, Action #5

www.books2read.com/MeetCute

ALSO BY ELISE FABER

Billionaire's Club **(all stand alone)**

Bad Night Stand

Bad Breakup

Bad Husband

Bad Hookup

Bad Divorce

Bad Fiancé

Bad Boyfriend

Bad Blind Date

Bad Wedding

Bad Engagement (October 12th, 2020)

Bad Swipe (March 1st, 2021)

Love, Action, Camera (all stand alone)

Dotted Line

Action Shot

Close-Up

End Scene

Meet Cute (April 5th, 2021)

Love After Midnight **(all stand alone)**

Rum and Notes

Virgin Daiquiri

On The Rocks (September 27th, 2020)

Between the Seats (April 2021)

***Gold Hockey* (all stand alone)**

Blocked

Backhand

Boarding

Benched

Breakaway

Breakout

Checked

Coasting

Centered

Charging (December 28th, 2020)

Caged (March 2021)

***Life Sucks Series* (all stand alone)**

Train Wreck

Hot Mess

Dumpster Fire (February 15th, 2021)

***Roosevelt Ranch Series* (all stand alone, series complete)**

Disaster at Roosevelt Ranch

Heartbreak at Roosevelt Ranch

Collision at Roosevelt Ranch

Regret at Roosevelt Ranch

Desire at Roosevelt Ranch

***Phoenix Series* (read in order)**

Phoenix Rising

Dark Phoenix

Phoenix Freed

***Phoenix: LexTal Chronicles* (rereleasing soon, stand alone, Phoenix world)**

From Ashes

To Smoke (January 25th, 2021)

In Flames

KTS Series

Fire and Ice (Hurt Anthology, stand alone)

Riding The Edge (December 7th, 2020)

Stand Alones

Someday, Maybe (YA)

ABOUT THE AUTHOR

USA Today bestselling author, Elise Faber, loves chocolate, Star Wars, Harry Potter, and hockey (the order depending on the day and how well her team -- the Sharks! -- are playing). She and her husband also play as much hockey as they can squeeze into their schedules, so much so that their typical date night is spent on the ice. Elise changes her hair color more often than some people change their socks, loves sparkly things, and is the mom to two exuberant boys. She lives in Northern California. Connect with her in her Facebook group, the Fabinators or find more information about her books at www.elisefaber.com.

facebook.com/elisefaberauthor
amazon.com/author/elisefaber
bookbub.com/profile/elise-faber
instagram.com/elisefaber
goodreads.com/elisefaber
pinterest.com/elisefaberwrite

Manufactured by Amazon.ca
Bolton, ON